THE
DISCOVERY

NOVELS BY HARRY KATZAN JR

The Mysterious Case of the Royal Baby

The Curious Case of the Royal Marriage

The Auspicious Case of the General and the Royal Family

A Case of Espionage

Shelter in Place

The Virus

The Pandemic

Life is Good

The Vaccine

A Tale of Discovery

FOREWORD

We live in untimely times and the title of this book reflects those times. The COVID-19 virus attacked the world in the spring of 2020. It is a pandemic and it took most people by surprise. History will say that it originated in China and spread from there to the rest of civilized society. This book is about the pandemic and some of the events that preceded and followed it. It is a novel and should be accorded all of the rights and privileges normally attained thereto.

This book was written during the pandemic when most persons were quarantined to mediate the ominous threat of the virus. The virus is highly contagious and people were encouraged to maintain a social distance from other individuals when out in the general public, and to stay indoors when possible. The wearing of facemasks was advised, and many people wore gloves and protective clothing, as well. Medical supplies and first responders were in short supply, and the death rate was high for a sickness of its kind. A vaccine was developed to prevent being infected by the virus, since no medicine was developed to directly cure persons once they were unlucky enough to come down to it.

The symptoms of the virus, referred to as coronavirus, are fever, dry cough, and tiredness and ironically, 80% of persons that recover from the disease recover without receiving special treatment. Older people, and people with other medical conditions, such as asthma, diabetes, or heart disease, may be more susceptible to becoming severely ill. More men contract COVID-19 than women. People that have contracted the disease may be sick 1 to 14 days before developing symptoms. In severe cases, sick persons may have difficulty breathing.

Protection against the virus involves personal hygiene and good respiratory behavior. Most municipalities adopt a slogan such as "Go home, Stay home." Thus, persons are advised to shelter in place by staying home except when absolutely necessary to go out among the general population. Preventative hygiene is recommended even though a person has received the vaccine.

Many persons were and are quarantined against the disease and the workplace is affected, since people are kept from work, resulting in financial difficulty. Social events involving 10 persons or more are cancelled and education is disrupted. Because older persons, who are most susceptible to the disease, are particularly at risk, special store hours are offered for them. When appropriate, food and supplies can be picked up at a supply center or are specially delivered. The medical facilities of a country with a COVID-19 outbreak are often taxed to the absolute limit, and first responders are frequently at a high risk. The medical profession is preparing additional medicines and vaccines to deal with the disease. Thank goodness for the efforts of all persons that have dealt with the problems associated with the disease.

The author,
March 15, 2021

PREFACE

Matt Miller and Ashley Wilson were friends. They initially met in Dr. Marguerite Purgoine's creative writing course, and usually got together afterwards at Starbucks to discuss life's never-ending set of problems, as students commonly do. After completing their university studies, Matt became an established mathematician and a prize winning golfer. Ashley had been a person seeking celebrity status. Dr. Purgoine, known personally as Anna for some unknown reason, was a distinguished professor and award-winning author. Matt's grandfather, Les Miller, was a retired general in the U.S. Air Force, and subsequently the founder of an influential political polling company. He was referred to as "the General," because of his collection of major accomplishments. The General was wealthy and liked to help people. This led to several interesting adventures for Matt and the General, often involving Ashley.

Like most persons in the modern world, they were hit by the Pandemic of 2020 as the worst thing that has ever happened to them. Words like shelter in place, facial mask, social distance, and wash our hands for 20 seconds are commonplace. Businesses, restaurants, bars, movie houses, sporting events are totally, if not partially, changed, and many people think our way of life in modern countries will never return.

COVID-19 is the name of the pandemic that took most people by surprise. History will say that it originated in China and spread from there to the rest of civilized society. The virus is highly contagious, and people were encouraged to maintain a social distance from other individuals when out in public and to stay indoors when possible. The wearing of facemasks was advised, and many people wore gloves and protective clothing. Medical supplies and first responders were in short supply, and the death rate was high for a sickness of its kind. In the beginning, there was no vaccine to prevent the virus, and no medicines to cure persons, once they were unlucky enough to attract it. Later, a vaccine was developed.

But, we're getting ahead of the story. What is a pandemic and where did the term come from? To begin, where did the terminology start? An *endemic* is sickness that belongs to a particular people or country, and an *outbreak* is a greater-than-anticipated increase in the number of endemic cases. If an outbreak is not controlled, it is called an *epidemic*. Lastly, a *pandemic* is an epidemic that spreads over multiple countries or continents and affects a large number of people. The sequence is *outbreak > epidemic > pandemic > endemic*.

Government leaders are concerned with pandemics from several different points of view. The most important point of view is clearly how to identify it, cure it, and prevent it. The source is very important, as well as how it affects various groups of people. Eventually, scientists get around to whether it is natural or man-made, and if so, who did it.

This novel attempts to answer some of these questions through the common form of entertainment known as a novel.

Matt and the General have an outstanding reputation as leaders of a team that can solve hard problems not assigned to normal organizations. Other problems within the domain of the pandemic involve the Royal Family and the U.S. White House.

CHARACTERS IN THE NOVEL

The General – Les Miller. Former military General and Humanitarian. P-51 pilot and war hero. Has bachelors, masters, and doctorate degrees.

Matthew (Matt) Miller – Professor of Mathematics. Has PhD degree. Grandson of the General.

Ashley Wilson Miller – College friend of Matt Miller. Former Duchess of Bordeaux. Married to Matt Miller. Has Master's degree and is a Receiver of the National Medal of Freedom.

Amelia Robinson – Citizen of the United States and former mole working for the United States and Russia. Has a PhD from studies in Russia.

Marguerite Purgoine - Retired creative writing Professor and an associate of the team. Has PhD degree. Known as Anna for some unknown reason.

Sir Charles (Buzz) Bunday – P-51 pilot. Army Air Force buddy of Les Miller. Member of the British Security Service. Knight of the United Kingdom.

Harper (Harp) Thomas – Professor of Mathematics at ETH. Buddy of Matt's in graduate school. Has PhD degree in mathematics.

Kimberly Jobsen Thomas – Consultant to a Swiss Bank. Married to Harper Thomas. Has masters degree in business.

Sir Prince Michael (Davis) – Duke of Bordeaux. Professor of Astrophysics. Knight of the United Kingdom. Has PhD degree in astrophysics.

Katherine Penelope Radford – Retired Queen of the United Kingdom. Queen Elizabeth II.

Kenneth Strong – President of the United States.

Alexi Belov – Russian mathematician.

Dimitri Aplov – Russian virologist.

And Others

PART I

TO ZÜRICH

1

THE TEAM GETS TOGETHER

The sky was blue, the breeze was balmy, and life was good for the General. He had been watching TV and reading USA Today on his cell phone, and things did not look good for the common people in America. The pandemic had surged and the upcoming Thanksgiving and Christmas holidays were forecast to raise the infection rate even more. There were 2,000 new infections in one day in November. Practically every news source advised travelers to stay home and emphasized facemasks, social distancing, and hand washing. Most people realized that a large number of travelers would ignore the social predictions, and be susceptible to the virus. Many would be hospitalized, and some of them would die.

The General called Matt and invited he and his wife Ashley to dine in the Green Room Restaurant that he owned. The restaurant had been primed as a defense against the coronavirus for more than a year. He would be bringing his friend, the retired professor Mme. Purgoine, known as Anna for some unknown reason.

The group dined in a special upstairs dining room that was cleaned regularly against the virus. The group removed their masks in order to talk and eat.

Matt initiated the conversation. "Hello everyone. It's been some time since we got together. Almost everyone that I know has been sheltering in place because of the virus."

No one said a word. They were used to not talking very much. Finally Anna replied, "I think we're here to talk about the coronavirus. What else is there to discuss? We rarely see or speak to anyone. I've finished all of my writing plans."

"So have I," said Ashley.

"I admit that I have finished my work, as well," said Matt. "I wrote a paper for a conference, and it was completed in record time. I'm teaching all of my courses online, and my PhD student meets with me via email."

"Is there anything we can do?" asked the General. "We have the three needed resources, time, brains, and money. We have been very successful in the past."

"One of the questions that has never been truly resolved, at least in my mind, is where did this virus come from?" continued the General. "Now we will have another outbreak with the same unanswered questions, where did the virus come from? We do not even know if it is the same virus. Last time, we were able to give answers that satisfied the President. Our friend Amelia was able to help us in that regard, and we hypothesized that the Russian spy procedure was, in fact, the source of the virus. If you remember Sir Michael, the leader of the successful Oxford vaccine solution, maintained that the source was airborne and possibly from outer space."

"That's true," said Ashley. "He was never successful in convincing anyone of his ideas."

"All that I remember," said the General, "is that practically everyone we talked to was more interested in the solution, which was the vaccine. Now that they have that aspect of the problem resolved, we can look into the long term solution."

"Michael had some interesting ideas," said Matt. "Just because his ideas were not mainstream, doesn't mean they were faulty."

"Now they are mostly interested in storage, distribution, and the cost of the vaccine," said Anna. "The major pharmaceuticals want profits, even though the U.S. government has funded almost everything, so far. I read yesterday evening that the Oxford version would cost something like fifty cents per dose and the American version would be between three and four dollars. The numbers I give are not necessarily correct but are somewhere in the neighborhood."

"We have assets all over the place – well not exactly all over – that we call on," said Ashley. "We have Sir Bunday, Harp Thomas, and his wife Kimberly. The Swiss and the English always seem to know what's going on. Do we have to call Sir Charles by his royal name?"

"I think he would prefer Buzz," answered the General.

"We don't know very much about the virus or talk to anyone that works on it, "said Ashley. "All we have is TV, iPhone messages, email, and newspapers."

3

"If I may add," added Matt. "news sources choose their sources, based on the journalistic objective. So you cannot exactly believe everything you hear or read."

"The only service we can depend on is the military," added the General. "Let me try to get some information from the Pentagon. We should meet in a few days and compare notes. Is a week too long and how many days is too short?

"Let's meet in four days," said Matt. "Some of us have courses and related activities to take care of."

"Any comments?" asked the General. "Okay, we will meet in four days."

As the group walked out, they were not visible from the dining area. Matt said to Ashley, "It seems strange not to have someone looking at us."

"It is strange," commented Ashley. "I kind of like it."

"You're a natural performer," said Matt.

On the way home, Matt asked Ashley if she had any of those easy solutions on what the team should do, if anything. "Not a one," said Ashley.

"The same with me," said Matt.

The General and Anna stopped in at the University Club for a nightcap. Both were surprisingly quiet. "You're quiet," said the General finally.

"I just don't have anything to talk about," answered Anna. "The virus and pandemic seem to be finally resolved, and all we have left is the increase in infections that is predicted to occur between Thanksgiving and Christmas. I do have a question. When two separate people get the virus, do they get the same kind of virus? I mean two people that are physically far apart."

"I don't have a clue," replied the General. "That is a very good question. I think I should check it out in the Pentagon."

"You seem to have liked the military," said Anna.

"I guess so," said the General. "I have pleasant memories. I think I changed things that effectively made a difference."

"I am sure you did," said Anna with a smile.

2

THE FOLLOWING DAY

Matt's online courses went like a breeze. Matt had given an online presentation the previous week, and used the current class to go over the student's last homework and give a brief review of the subject. Another hour exam was right around the corner. He had some free class time, so he asked the following question of the class, "I'm kind of interested in this COVID business. Could you ladies and gentlemen give me some of your thoughts on the subject? Maybe there is an interesting math problem in what you come up with. We've spent the entire term, so far, on purely theoretical topics, and a brief diversion could be interesting. You don't have to do this, but perhaps you, as being good math students, might come up with something interesting."

"Here is what I was thinking," wrote one student. "Maybe one person has the virus and can pass it on. Possibly, in one or more cases, the available recipient doesn't accept it, because his or her immune system blocks it, or the recipient has taken the vaccine. How do you distinguish one case from another? What about the case of a person who is asymptomatic, but can pass it on. Is there such a thing as an asymptomatic strain of the virus? Maybe the vaccine only works under certain circumstances like when there is a full moon. Maybe the virus spores come from outer space and some get damaged having had to travel several light years to get here. Then some would work and others would not. Maybe the virus is airborne and comes from those Saudi clouds that seem to pop up every year."

"It's a differential equation," wrote another student on his Internet connection to Matt.

"Are you referring to how the virus spreads?" answered Matt.

"Yes," wrote the student. "Doesn't the spread of a disease have to deal with rate of change."

Always the gentleman, Matt responded. "I'll have to give that some thought. It's a good start."

"Anyone else?" asked Matt.

No one answered, so Matt terminated the online class.

In the graduate class, no one responded to Matt's query, and Matt did not mention the subject to his PhD candidate.

After class, Matt got a call from the General. He said, "Hi Matt. How's it going?"

Matt knew in a moment that the General had something in mind, and it involved doing something that he probably didn't necessarily want to do.

"Things are fine," replied Matt. "I presented our problem of the source of the virus to my students and got a couple of interesting responses."

"If they are promising, then we should take a look at them," said the General. "By the way, can you fly us to Langley tomorrow. It would be a one-day trip."

"Does this trip have something to do with our talk to someone at the Pentagon that you mentioned?" asked Matt.

"It does," said the General. "I talked to Mark Clark. You remember he was Chairman of the Joint Chiefs of Staff. He's retired now and is interested in the pandemic. Actually, he was at home, but the Pentagon will always be our place of residence."

"Let me think," said Matt. "I think I've got it. Does this have anything to do with the drug named Hydroxychloroguine that the military has an enormous supply of and the President has taken for whatever reason?"

"It does," replied the General. "How did you figure that one out?"

"It was easy," answered Matt with a grin on his face. "I just ran through all of the options and ideas we have heard, and it was the only one that made sense. Remember, the easiest solution is often the best one. When do we leave and what should I wear?"

"I'll pick you up at 8:30 am and wear a dark suit, white shirt, and black shoes. We will fly to Langley, and a military limo will take us to the Pentagon. Do you still have your military ID from that extraction operation in London?"

"I still have it," replied Matt. "I was a colonel."

"Bring it, and I'll explain everything on the flight," answered the General. "I changed my mind. Wear the uniform."

"How did you know that I was free and that I would do it?" asked Matt.

"You have freedom with your online courses, and I can always depend on you."

"Thanks, Sir," said Matt.

When Ashley heard about the trip to the Pentagon, she wasn't at all happy. "Do you really have to do this?" she said. "What is the benefit to you? And maybe you will have a plane crash. You know that it happens. When a small plane is involved, you just don't hear about them. Why doesn't the General just settle down and do something with Anna?"

"I just think I should do this," said Matt. "I'm a good pilot, and our plane is failure proof."

"What about the other plane in a crash?" said Ashley. "Maybe the other pilot won't be so good."

Matt ignored Ashley's comment. "Our plane is failure proof, and it can land itself. Also, with two experienced pilots onboard, the chance of a problem is infinitesimal."

"Sooner or later, you are going to have a problem," said Ashley. "This flying all over the place has to be corralled."

"Actually, you are right," replied Matt, "Would you like to fly with us? I'll ask the General. I'm sure he will not mind."

"It would be nice to go, but I don't want you to get in trouble with the General. He could chew you out."

"No, he won't because we know each other and trust each other," said Matt. "I'll ask him right now."

Matt called the General. His only response was, "Why not. Tell her to wear her uniform and bring her military ID card. I believe she was a Major."

Matt told Ashley, and all she said was, "I'm sorry I brought it up. I should keep my mouth shut."

"We'd like to have you with us," continued Matt. "The General likes you, and he might need some help with decision making. You have to wear your Army uniform and bring your Army ID card. Do you remember what you were?"

"I was a Major," said Ashley, "The first time I was a Captain. What are you?"

"I was a Colonel," answered Matt. "I hope no one asks us a question we can't answer."

"Just say it's classified," said Ashley. "That's the easiest solution."

"Remember, the military ID has to match the uniform," added Matt.

"Do I need a special haircut?" asked Ashley.

"Don't know," said Matt. "You're a Major, so I suppose you can do what you want. Don't wear high heels."

"I bet I'd get some attention," said Ashley.

"They have an entertainment place in the basement with coffee, diet Coke, and things to eat," said Matt. "There is no charge, but of course, we really pay for it in our taxes."

3

THE PENTAGON

The General picked up Matt and Ashley at 8:30 am as planned. The trip to the local airport took 10 minutes and their private aircraft was already running, and the flight plan was recorded. Flying into the DC area was controlled by the military, and the General had permission to fly at 500 mph at 50,000 feet.

In minutes, they were airborne. Matt and the General were in the pilot and the co-pilot seats, respectively. Ashley sat in the passenger area. The General made an immediate request, "We have plenty of time and things to discuss, so can we set the speed at 400 miles per hour and the elevation to 40,000 feet?"

"Yes, Sir," said Matt, who turned around to Ashley and smiled, as if to say, 'He's probably scared'. Matt set the autopilot accordingly, and said, "You mentioned that you would tell us why we are going to visit the Pentagon, and it has, as you have said to me, something to do with the medicine named Hydroxychloroquine."

"It is a very easy question to answer," said the General. "As you probably know, malaria is a terrible problem in occupied Africa. Medical scientists have discovered a successful antidote called Hydroxychloroquine. It has reduced the death rate from malaria in Africa to practically zero. We have thousands of troops in Africa, and we have stockpiled the medicine for their protection.

"I think I read about it," said Matt. "Isn't it supposed to protect against all types of infectious diseases by strengthening the taker's immune system? Is that why the President took it?"

"Well, you never really know why people do things," answered the General, "But I think it was to show that the administration is doing something about the pandemic."

"What is your military friend Mark Clark up to?" asked Matt. "Is he involved with the Hydroxychloroquine medicine? Oh, another question. Do you expect to get a shot of it while we are in the Pentagon? Should Ashley and I expect to get one also? I suppose it would do no harm."

"I did plan to get a shot and the two of you can get one also," said the General. "It is up to you. It is not a vaccine or an antidote. It is just something to condition your immune system to be stronger, as you said."

"I guess I'll plan on getting one of those shots," said Matt. "Ashley can also take a shot if she wants to."

"I'm in," said Ashley.

"That isn't the only reason we have come this far," continued Matt. "You must have something else in the back of your mind."

"There is," replied the General. "I think we should get involved with this pandemic situation and don't know where to start. I realize that you investigated the Russian possibility as a source of worldwide proliferation, but that seems too simple for me. It may have pleased the President, but it doesn't please me. The military looks into everything, and is a good place to start. Clark has an inquisitive mind. That's why I wanted to meet with him. He's also easy to get along with, which is important when a person is in search of information."

The plane landed smoothly, since Matt was an experienced pilot and took pride in doing everything perfectly. On the way to the entry terminal, Matt asked the General how fast was the P-51. The General said that the speed of the P-51 was 423 mph and had a distance of almost one thousand miles that was good for World War II. He mentioned that he thought the B-52 flew at about 600 mph but didn't remember exactly.

"I've read that with large aircraft, the pilot drives the plane like one drives an automobile. But with fighter planes, such as the P-51, and perhaps the modern F-22, the pilot flies as though the plane were an extension of himself," added Matt.

The General remarked that he thought that was true. He remarked that flying a large aircraft like the B-29 or B-52 was like driving a luxury automobile, and a fighter was like driving a sports car.

"It's really a pleasure talking to you, Sir," said Matt.

"We always talked like that," said the General. "It's one of the pleasures of my life. As you can imagine, I could never talk to Anna, for example, like that. She probably wouldn't understand, and for sure she wouldn't care."

The military limo ride to the Pentagon was slow and boring. The General reminded Matt and Ashley that they shouldn't say anything important in the limo, as they might be recorded. He didn't think so, but you never know. The highways were congested and the driver seemed to be overly cautious. Matt said that if he were driving a four-star general with his chest filled with ribbons and medals, he would be extra careful. When a four-star general appeared in public, it was mandatory to wear his or her dress uniform with all relevant insignias. Matt and Ashley wore dress uniforms, but insignias were not necessary.

The guards at the Pentagon were exceedingly courteous and waved the general and his companions through without concern. The General had a smile on his face and said to Matt and Ashley, "Rank still has its privileges."

Retired four-star General Mark Clark had an honorary office in the restricted area of the outside ring of the sixth floor. The General did not feel that Matt and Ashley would be permitted into that area, so he recommended the coffee shop on the ground floor where they could relax. The food and drink were free of charge, but apparel and other purchases were offered at a relatively low price. The lower floors were guarded by Marines in dress uniforms and armed with automatic weapons. Even the General did not know what was going on down there.

As the three were walking along the ground floor, an unexpected event occurred. They passed a group of Army Reservists, and one of them said to Matt. "Don't I know you? You are one of the professors."

Matt looked up and it was a student from the university. He was not a math student, but Matt recognized the face from the hallways. Matt was quick; should he be the brother or the cousin?

"Well, hi," said Matt. "He's my cousin. We look alike. He's the smart one. This is our grandfather, the General, and the Major is my wife, Kathy. We were at a wedding and just dropped in to see how the facility has changed."

The young reservist looked at the general with all the decorations, a Major, and a Colonel, and was overwhelmed beyond belief. The General said, "It is a pleasure meeting you, young fellow. Enjoy your visit."

The reservist quickly walked off, and the General said, "Well done Matt. You did exactly the most appropriate thing."

The Reservist said to his Captain, "I shouldn't have said anything."

The Reserve Captain answered, "In the Army, it is always better to speak only when you are addressed. You've learned a lesson."

As they walked away, Matt said, "Hi Kathy." Ashley gave him an elbow and the General just smiled.

4

MEETING WITH GENERAL CLARK

The General knocked at the door of Mark Clark's office on the outside ring of the sixth floor and received the customary "Come in."

"Hello, Mark" said the General. "How are you doing?"

"Not too bad," said Mark Clark, a Four-Star General and former Chairman of the Joint Chiefs of Staff. "Feeling a little older these days, but still able to go with the best."

"How's the missus?" asked the General.

"She's as good as gold," said Clark. "Do you still miss yours?"

"I sure do," answered the General. "When a person dies of cancer, everyone feels it. I have a retired professor of creative writing who keeps me company, but she is just a placeholder who is someone to talk to and that's about it. My grandson, Matt, the math professor, is about the only one I can talk to. His wife is very good looking, and it's a pleasure to have dinner with the two of them. I always bring my retired friend, and we are two handsome couples."

"Any interesting projects going on?' asked Clark.

"No, and that is why I am here," replied the General. "I feel that we can help with some aspect of the pandemic, but I can't get a handle on anything specific. We uncovered that Russian operation where spy trainees spread the virus, and then the scientist died before he could develop a vaccine and be awarded a Nobel Prize, which he dearly wanted. The President liked it, and it quieted some of his opponents in the population, but that solution is too simple for me. The world has been working on the pandemic vaccine, and I guess it will be successful. The question of the where, how, and what of the virus have yet to be determined. There seems to be a whole host of unanswered questions about that subject, related to the nature of the underlying virus."

"You've got a good point there," said Clark. "It seems as though the military has absolutely no interest as to where the virus came from, and that subject could be a national security component. The pandemic virus is often called the Chinese virus by some people, and others say that couldn't be true because of the outbreak in the city of Wuhan, and the Chinese people would not like to endanger their own people. Please excuse me if that name is not exactly correct. Well, all I have to say is that the government in some countries does not care that much about people's lives, so they could have been testing the virus on their own people. I do have a small bit of information for you. Remember the story that the outbreak of the virus came from bats, and Chinese eat bats. That is why the virus had been given the name 'Chinese

Virus'. At least, that is what some people say. Actually, bats do carry viruses and the Chinese do eat them, but apparently there is no valid connection between them. It doesn't seem logical that a bunch of two-inch bats could cause all the loss of life that is supposedly caused by the so-called Chinese virus. Some female virologist has a computer description of it, and the Chinese government went to the World Health Organization (WHO), and had it registered as a virus. The virus was only in the computer and nowhere else, and the scientist suddenly vanished. The computer virus even has an official identification that I'll give you before you leave. You know how it is with the international organization WHO. Give them a few million dollars and they will say anything. Some people, namely our President, still call the pandemic virus the Chinese virus. Here are the names. The scientist's name is Dr. Shir and the ID for the virus is Ratg13. So that is the end of the bat theory."

"You can't trust anyone, it seems," said the General.

"You are probably here to find out what I think about the situation," continued Clark. "So here it is. After a little less than one year, we do not know how the virus came about, when it occurred, and where. All of these virologists floating around in the world are totally worthless. They are, of course, better now, and we will probably have a vaccine soon, but that is what I think. The U.S. should be taking the lead with regard to the pandemic, and it isn't"

"What is happening in the Pentagon?" asked the General.

"We have a pretty boy and a team working on it, and all they have come up with are the results given in the reports generated by your team, and in particular, the work of a

Madame Purgoine. Internally to the Pentagon, your people are heroes, especially that Dr. Matt who is fancied by the White House.

The General and Mark Clark reminisced about the 'good old days" in the military, and the General left for the coffee break room.

"Let's have lunch," said the General to Matt and Ashley. "I think the Mayflower Hotel would be a good place. We can discuss things and then head on home."

5

RETURN TO NEW JERSEY

The Mayflower is a grand hotel in the capital district that grew in prestige as the United States emerged as a world-class power. Matt and Ashley had never been there before, but the General was a regular from his days in active military service. The maitre'd, named Dominic, greeted the team with superlatives. The luncheon area was packed with diners, but there was always room for a Four-Star General, who ordered his usual filet mignon with all the trimmings along with a couple of scotches. Matt and Ashley had tilapia fish with no drink. The General did not mention his meeting with General Clark, and Matt was obviously curious. They were both playing some unknown men's game, so Ashley took the situation in her own hands.

"My dear General," said Ashley. "Did you by chance have the opportunity to converse with your intended host?" She thought and rightly so that, *little boys love to play games.*

"I did, indeed," said the General. "He was complimentary of the work of our team, especially the writing of Anna. You are heroes, and he hoped we could continue, I assume. There was very little specificity in our conversation. He mentioned the origin of the Chinese virus situation, but he offered no specific needs and no suggestions. The name 'Chinese virus' is a result of a non-existent virus by a non-existent researcher by the name of Dr. Shir. He reminded me of that story by a well-known computer scientist who was forming an Artificial Intelligence (AI) group for some organization. A young fellow was assigned to the team, and the computer scientist asked him what he had done in the field of AI. The fellow said he knew nothing, but said he was interested in the concept. General Clark was that young fellow on the subject of the pandemic. The information about the virus was sent to the World Health Organization, and the scientist was never seen or heard from again. The virus was only a computer description and nothing more."

"So we got nothing out of this trip to the Pentagon," said Matt.

"That would appear to be the case," replied the General. "Other than the nice luncheon that we are now enjoying."

"That's the way most business and scientific advances go," said Matt. "There always is a ramp-up process, often with missteps, that a project goes through. I wouldn't be too concerned about the current situation."

"Well spoken," said the General. "Since Clark is a long-time friend of mine, I thought we could get a lot more out of him."

"For what?" asked Matt. "We haven't even specified a need for high-powered talent. Perhaps, he recognized there was no slot for him and regarded it as a sign of trouble."

"You've got a good point," said the General. "Let's enjoy the meal, and discuss the situation on our flight home."

"This is a well-designed hotel," said Ashley. "My father used to talk about it. It's a little old, but it has modern features and a lot of amenities. Does this dining room have a name?"

"I think it is called the Edgar Bar & Kitchen," said the General. "Overall, the hotel has had a few scandals – if you want to call them that – but none serious enough to tarnish its good name. It was founded in the 1920s."

"It must be profitable," added Matt. "If it weren't, they would have replaced it by now. I personally think it is a very nice place, and the location is ideal."

"People are looking at us," said Matt. "It's just like the Green Room. You would think they would have something to talk about, but they don't."

"I suppose that is because we are pleasant to look at," said Ashley. "Maybe they think you are the four-star general having dinner with his son and daughter – also in uniform."

"They are thinking that the father is how the children got to be officers," added Matt.

"I doubt that," said the General. "You've forgotten that I am a the grandfather."

"You don't look like a grandfather," replied Ashley. "You do look like our father, especially you and Matt do with your golf suntan and lean figures."

"Thanks for being so nice to us," said the General.

"You're usually the persons being nice – to me," said Ashley.

"Don't get too carried away with that," interrupted Matt. "We're being watched. See that couple on our left. The lady has a Dooney & Bourke purse on the table. It's got a directional receiver, and it is pointed to the general. They're very interested in what we are saying, and how we are acting. They watched us when we were seated. The man is trying not to look like he is watching us, and the woman was too busy arranging her purse on the table. They are not that smart. The purse is a Dooney & Bourke model and the receiving side has been modified for the receiver and the camera. Normally, a man is ill mannered and just looks at you, and a woman doesn't protect her bag in a place like this. And if she did, she wouldn't adjust it. She can record the two of you but not me, since I am facing the other way. I chose the seats with that in mind when we came in."

"How do you know all of this," said the General with his hand over his mouth.

"I don't specifically try to do it," said Matt. "When I walk into a room, I just see everything without specifically appearing to do so. You know this."

"What's the deal on the purse?" asked Ashley. "How do you know about it?"

"From QVC," answered Matt. "I bought one for my mother for Christmas."

"What's QVC?" asked the General.

"I think it is Quality Value Channel," said Matt.

That spoiled the conversation, which then drifted on to the NFL and the rearranging of football games because of the virus, and who would win the Super Bowl.

6

THE FLIGHT HOME

The military limo trip from Washington to Langley was largely uneventful. The team felt they were probably being recorded so they spoke very little, and what they did say was trivial. The General was disappointed with his friend General Mark Clark, because his expectations were not met in any sense of the word. Matt thought that a few setbacks was an integral part of doing research and was not concerned at all. Ashley showed no emotions whatsoever. Her attitude was, whatever will be will be.

On the plane trip home, things got more interesting. The General sat in the co-pilot's seat and tried to run the show. His range of interests went from how to fly the plane to his plans for solving the pandemic problem for the next ten years.

Matt expressed an interest in what the Russians were doing and decided his method of entry into Russia would be best through the math department, in general, and the upcoming math conference at the ETH conference on math and astrophysics coming up the next week in Zürich. He had a paper prepared on *A Topological Analysis of Dark Matter in Non-Euclidean Hyperspace*, and decided to call the program chairman, who was his friend from previous mathematical discoveries. He would allow a last minute entry of a paper. He had another paper on AI developed mathematical structures, but the results were beyond human consumption at this stage. The General said he would like to check into the nature of pandemic viruses in England, and in particular, would like to talk to Sir Michael at Oxford, the leader of the English project that developed the Pfizer/BioNTech's highly anticipated coronavirus vaccine. The General had expressed a profound interest in the attributes of the virus, such as its distribution in diverse countries, origin of a virus, different viruses and mutations, projects in the U.S. Russia, England, and wherever else research is being performed. Ashley was more specific and probably specific enough to yield useful results. She said she was interested in the nature of viruses, immunization, and vaccines – regardless of where and how they occur. She said she felt it was important to know precisely what constituted a virus.

Matt was the most productive of the three. He was quick to request a clarification from the team and give his opinion and advice. The group was stymied with what to do with Anna, until Matt came up with the need for case studies that could be available through the media. When they landed in New Jersey, a complete project plan was in order. Ashley had to use the restroom in the airport, and Matt asked the

General if he would be seeing the retired queen in England. The General said that he hadn't made any specific plans but that was a distinct possibility. Matt was pleased to hear that. The General worked hard and needed some sort of reward for his hard work.

Matt and Ashley were both glad to get back to their teaching duties. The General called Anna to arrange a dinner in the Green Room. Life was good.

Matt made his arrangements to attend the math conference the next week, and Ashley ordered a book on immunization from the college bookstore. Matt probably could have found one in the university library for her, but Ashley wanted to do it on her own. If the General or Matt knew about the order, they would have been pleased. As it turned out, the book was delivered to Ashley at home.

While the team was in Washington, the President was taken to the Walter Reed Military Medical Center with a case of COVID-19. He was tested positive for the virus and has been given a variety of drugs to ease the effects of the virus and reduce his recovery time. He was administered a cocktail of drugs that are being tested and not available to the general public. The drugs that had been given are:

> Dexamethasone – This is a steroid normally used to treat asthma, arthritis, and cancer. The President's blood oxygen level had dropped and was prescribed for severe cases of COVID-19.

Remdesivir – This a drug used to improve recovery time by targeting coronaviruses ability to replicate themselves.

Regeneron's Monoclonal Antibody – This drug reduces the level of the virus in patients when given early.

Zinc – Used to fight outside bacteria and viruses.

Vitamin D – Used to reduce inflammation.

Famotidine – This is a drug used to reduce the amount of acid in the stomach.

Melatonin – Used to treat insomnia in obese and diabetic patients.

Aspirin – Used to prevent heart disease in older patents. COVID-19 can trigger blood clots and aspirin reduces the risk.

The President was out in a few days with good results and his case was closed. Ashley had some input to work on, and the team was pleased.

7

PLANNING

The stage was set for a flurry of activity from the team of Matt, the General, and Ashley. Matt had the most to do, and his level of planning was the most complex. First thing was to call the program chairman at Stanford to get on the math conference program. Matt was fortunate that the chairman had yet to make up the schedule and had not sent the papers to the printer for printing. Most conferences had online programs, but not mathematics. Attendees liked to have a printed program and proceedings that served two main purposes. One advantage is that an attendee could read up on a subject to get the most out of a presentation. The second was to discourage attendees that didn't understand the subject matter. Matt and the chairman from Stanford liked each other and could understand each other and ended up spending two hours discussing important things in mathematics. They agreed to meet at the James Joyce pub on their day of arrival. The time of the meeting was open. The chairman didn't even have a hotel reservation, so he agreed to call Matt at the zum Storchen when he got to Zürich. Next, Matt thought about calling another friend, Dr. Alexi Belov, a mathematician from Lomonosov Moscow State University, who was as westernized as a Russian could be. He had longed to move to the United States to teach mathematics and do research at a top notch American University. From Matt's point of view, Alexi Belov, known as Al, was the best mathematician he had ever met. His English was impeccable, and he had fallen in love with the American game of golf. Then Matt remembered the time zones and decided to make the call at a later time. Matt approached the Provost about recruiting a person from Russia and received the following reply, "Matt, we told you five years ago that we needed a foreign faculty member to enrich our reputation as a first rate university. You can visit him in Russia, if you would like. Our Dean of Foreign Relations will handle the paper work. Just get us the person. We have connections in Washington at the State Department, and you will have the travel arrangements taken care of for you. You will need a visa and probably some other things."

Matt was more than pleased. He accessed the Internet in his university office to find out the time in Moscow. There is an eight-hour time difference, so Matt decided to call Al early the next morning. Matt thought it would be good for the university to have a top notch Russian mathematician on the faculty, but he was quick to remember that his overall objective was to obtain information on the virus situation in Russia. They had a working vaccine, and it would be beneficial to know how they had progressed so rapidly.

Perhaps, their success was based on the simple fact that they had invented the virus. You never know.

It was difficult to stay on track. The overall objective was to gain information on the Russian approach to the virus, and the reason he was going to contact Al was to get his help to meet the scientist in charge. It was even possible that the virus scientist might want to spend some time – possibly the rest of his career in the States. Matt needed a name, and almost without thinking decided to give Amelia Robinson a call in Ohio. He had her telephone number, as well as email and message addresses, in his private little black book. The call was direct, as the location was Ohio, and Ohioans never worried about trivia such as answering systems. Matt thought that it might be pleasant to live in Ohio. In New Jersey, there was always a ridiculous problem popping up. Matt made the call. Amelia answered on the first ring.

"Hi, Amelia. This is Matt."

"Matt, my favorite person in the whole world," said Amelia. "How are you doing?"

"I'm busy at the moment," said Matt. "Otherwise, things are back to normal. University work and eating at the Green Room are my primary activities. How about you?"

"The work of a Registrar is never finished," said Amelia. "It's like being an accountant, everything has to be accurate down to the last grade recorded. I think you are calling me for a reason."

"Well, yes," said Matt, "other than hearing your pleasant voice. It seems that Russia has done well with the virus and were the first in the world to have a vaccine. There also was the case of the scientist who developed the virus and came up with a plan to distribute it. Then, he died before he could develop the vaccine. We would like to talk with his assistant to analyze the characteristics of the virus and determine where it came from. We can even have someone go over there and talk with him."

"I know his name, which is Dimitri Aplov," answered Amelia. "He works at the Moscow State University."

"Is he the kind of guy who would talk to an American?" asked Matt.

"I suppose so," replied Amelia. "Some people said he did all the work, and his boss took all the credit. I think that in order to get to talk with him, you are going to have to have a Russian person make the connection. They are concerned with spies in Russia."

"Do you ever think about when you were a spy for Russia, and then for the U.S.?" asked Matt.

"No, not often," answered Amelia, "I'm financially comfortable, and I have more money than I can spend. Oh, one more thing. If someone comes over to speak with Aplov, have him come with his wife, or his girlfriend, as the case may be. They seem to think that spies do not have female company. Don't ask me why."

"Talking with you is like watching a good movie," said Matt. "I hope we can get together in some capacity."

"Me too," said Amelia. "As I said, you're the best."

8

CONFERENCE PREPARATION

Matt arose at 6:30 as usual. He was concerned about calling Alexi Belov, since he already might be heading to the math conference in Switzerland. Actually, both Alexi and Matt had attended the math conference for the last 4 years. Alexi was pleased with the conference and also the opportunity to come to the U.S. Matt said he would bring the paperwork and a summary of the other details in moving to the U.S. Matt was confident that the Dean of Foreign Relations would take care of any issues that arose. In their conversations, Matt specifically did not mention a possible meeting with the scientist Dimitri Aplov, a well-known virologist. He felt that aspect of the situation might take care of itself. Ashley had not awakened yet, so Matt called Harp Thomas in Zürich, Switzerland. They discussed the conference, and Harp mentioned that he would also be giving a paper. Harp mentioned something that immediately received Matt's complete attention. Harp had been working with a colleague who had developed a math model of the pandemic. Harp mentioned some real life simulations that had been run. In short, the projections for Switzerland and England did not match up, and they did not know why. Harp mentioned, as a joke, that the viruses might be different. They agreed to meet at the math conference in Zürich. Matt asked how Harp's wife, Kimberly, had adapted to the Swiss way, and Harp said she loved living there. Also, that she was pregnant.

Ashley had late classes and slept in. When she awakened, Matt asked her if she would like having breakfast at Starbucks. She readily agreed and off they went for their usual yogurt, scone, and coffee breakfast. They remembered their early meetings there, and both were in a good mood.

Matt mentioned the math conference and the Russia trip, and all Ashley said was that she wished she could go with him, and that would be good for the project. A loud bell rang in Matt's head, and he mentioned that a female companion could work to his advantage. Ashley had classes during the math conference, but was free afterwards because of fall break at her college. She had a light teaching load because of the pandemic, and the drama course did not lend itself to online teaching.

Matt asked Ashley how she was doing with the pandemic project, and she said that she had been busy and hadn't done a thing. Matt mentioned that she had to come up to speed as it was possible that they could meet with Dimitri Aplov, who was a well-known scientist. She said she would spend some time on the project, and both headed to their respective academic jobs.

When Matt got to the university, he called the Dean of Foreign Relations and requested a meeting to discuss Alexi Belov and possibly Dimitri Aplov.

The Dean of Foreign Relations was elated to see Matt, because this was his first opportunity to do something strategic for the university. Matt mentioned Ashley and the fact that couples were trusted and singles were often regarded as spies. The Dean agreed. All he said was that you had to spend money to get good people. Actually, because of his good reputation, Matt was effectively using the university to obtain entrance to the Russia system. Intellectually, he realized this is how the world operates, using one asset to obtain another. When you were doing it yourself, the process was cumbersome. He was recruiting Alexi for the university and also to obtain access to the virus expert. Russia was more of a closed society than the U.S., and he was going to use Ashley to facilitate whatever protocols were involved. The Dean was part of the plan as he could obtain needed paperwork, as required.

Preliminary plans for attending the math conference were complete. The General was anxious to get started with the new project and offered to fly Matt to Zürich, mentioning that he would take care of all the details of the trip. Matt said he needed a day to get ready, one day for the flight, and then the next day was the conference. The conference would last two days, and then there was the flight back to the States.

The General actually made arrangements for the pilots, the flight plan, and the hotel reservations at the zum Storchen Hotel in Zürich. He planned on one day for the flight to Switzerland, two days for the conference, and then the trip home. That was four days, two of which were occupied with flights, but what should he do in Switzerland? He thought of inviting Mme. Purgoine and spending some time in the small village of Klosters and the well-known restaurant named Chesa Creshuna, that he called Restaurant Chesa. Mme. Purgoine, known as Anna for some unknown reason, would like that the famous American novelist Irwin Shaw had written and lived in a chalet across the street from the Restaurant Chesa and had a reserved table in the restaurant. The best table in the house, however, was the one reserved for Deborah Kerr, the famous American actress. The notion of a reserved table for a celebrity was a means of attracting business, as the reserved table was otherwise available to the diners of the Restaurant Chesa. Reserved tables are customary in Switzerland. Even small restaurants would reserve lunch tables at the restaurant for next-door workers. Anna would admire the concept of conventions like reserved tables for celebrities.

9

ABOUT THE MATH CONFERENCE

While the annual math conference in Zürich, Switzerland did not exactly grab the front-page headlines in the newspapers of the world, it was the place to be for mathematicians and would be mathematicians. The location was excellent, and the subjects were always at the leading edge of their respective mathematical disciplines. Matt was looking forward to it. He had not missed a meeting since he earned his PhD. To many professors, it was the highlight of the academic year.

The General's Gulfstream 650 had left Newark International Airport at 10:00 pm and landed a little more than 6 hours later at Kloten Airport in Zürich. Matt, the General, and Anna were on board, having taken a short flight to Newark on a small plane, also owned by the General. The travelers took a taxi to the zum Storchen Hotel that was built along the side of the famous Limmat River that flows from the north into the Lake of Zürich. The pilots would follow after the Gulfstream was stowed. It was early morning, but the travelers were allowed to check into the zum Storchen. The General was a good customer. After a customary 5-hour nap, Matt went down to the front desk and checked his messages. There were two of them: one from the math conference program chairman, and the other from Alexi Belov. Each of them left a tentative time for the planned meeting at the James Joyce pub: the program chairman at 2:00 and Alexi at 4:00. Matt walked the half mile to the James Joyce pub on Pelikanstrasse enjoying the exercise.

Dr. William Roberts from Stanford University was already seated when Matt arrived. Roberts was the program chairman of the math conference. They had little to discuss, but were happy to see each other. They both loved all aspects of mathematics. Roberts mentioned a math equation for the description of virus propagation, and Matt wondered if that formula was used in the simulation known to Harp Thomas. Actually, Harp might already be involved with that project and know of the equation. Roberts gave Matt a copy of the latest book he had written and Matt felt sorry he had not brought one of his own to give to Roberts. He would make up for it after he returned home.

After the two mathematicians ended their conversation, Matt called Harp Thomas on his cell phone. "Come on over," said Harp. "I'm just across the Rennweg from you, if you are at the zum Storchen. Kimberly would like to see you. She's as big as a horse, and we should become parents soon – very soon."

"I'm at the James Joyce at the moment, so I'll be there in fifteen minutes," replied Matt.

HARRY KATZAN JR.

Matt took a leisurely stroll from the James Joyce to the apartment across the street from the hotel. Harp and Kimberly were happy to see Matt. It is always pleasant to meet with fellow Americans when in a foreign country.

"What do you think Matt?" asked Kimberly. "How would we do as a Mom and Dad?"

"I don't have any experience with that subject," answered Matt. "I'm sure everything will be absolutely fine, especially here in Switzerland."

"Are you going to the math conference?" asked Harp. "I guess you are. Otherwise you wouldn't be here."

"I'm giving a paper entitled *A Topological Analysis of Dark Matter in Non-Euclidean Hyperspace*," said Matt, "and to meet with Alexi Belov about coming to the States as a full time faculty member. I would like to talk to you about the results of your mathematical model for the pandemic virus. You said your results did not agree with reality, but is it accurate in some cases?"

"We are not virus specialists, but here is my view of it. A small piece of the vaccine is entered in the patients immune system to get it going," said Harp. "There is something going on there. It's almost as if there is more to it than only a simple strain of virus."

"I don't have a background in this subject either," said Matt. "Perhaps Alexi knows someone at Moscow University in that area. The Russians say they already have a vaccine. The Russians do not have the same safety protocols as the U.S., but that does not mean á priori that their methods are faulty."

"Maybe the vaccine is only for their type of virus," replied Harp. "You never know. That could explain a lot of things."

"I have a meeting with Alexi at the James Joyce in a few minutes," said Matt. "Perhaps, he will have something to say on the subject. I'll be seeing the two of you when the baby is born, but if I don't, good luck. You deserve the best."

Matt hurried up to Pelikanstrasse, and Alexi was sitting in the James Joyce bar in a banquette facing the door. The mathematicians shook hands. There was no hugging with Russians. Alexi ordered a white wine spritzer and Matt had a non-alcoholic beer.

The two friends discussed their personal lives and also their mathematical lives. Alexi was apprehensive. He was obviously waiting for something.

"We would like you to be a professor at my university," said Matt. "The appointment would be permanent, and the university and the U.S. State Department will make all arrangements, including coordination with the Russian government. The transfer will be totally above board. You will be given a date and a time for the flight to the U.S. You will probably be given an honorarium by both the Russian government and the United States government. Your salary will be at the highest level of full professor, and a residence will be provided for you in a luxury apartment for faculty and researchers. An associate will be assigned to help you until you get adjusted. Additionally, I will be responsible for your academic work and will handle your personal life."

Matt continued, "Do you accept the position?"

"Yes, I do," said Alexi.

Alexi had a broad smile on his face.

Alexi and Matt agreed to meet at the conference after Matt's presentation.

"We can have lunch at a fine establishment in Zürich," said Matt. "At that luncheon, I will have the formal paperwork available for you to sign. You will automatically be supplied with copies of all appropriate documentation."

"We are pleased to have you as an associate," said Matt, "and I am sure you will be pleased with the university. You will be treated with the highest honors a university can provide. Welcome to the United States."

10

THE CHESA GRISCHUNA IN KLOSTERS

The General and Mme. Purgoine had ridden along with Matt on the taxi ride from Kloten Airport to the zum Storchen Hotel. Mme. Purgoine, called Anna for some unknown reason, was totally fascinated with Switzerland. She had traveled extensively in Europe, Asia, and the United States, but Switzerland was new to her. Most Swiss spoke perfect English, but for some reason, had little interest in her work.

Anna and the General had a light breakfast at the Storchen upon arriving, and decided to take the five-hour sleep recommended for international travelers traveling east.

The General remembered a trip to Klosters for economics conferences, a small village with excellent visitor attractions, that he had visited in his Army days. He had stayed at the Chesa Grischuna and liked it, and asked the concierge at the Storchen to secure a reservation for two nights along with meals. A reservation was available, and the General proposed to Anna, a short stay in Klosters. She readily agreed.

The next morning, the General and Anna took a first-class train to Klostars. They had good Swiss bread and coffee aboard the train, and loved it. Anna was very interested in the scenery and talked up a storm. The General observed a Swiss couple doing the same. Between the lady's expressions, all the man could say was *ya-ya*. The General thought the Swiss needed a ya-ya machine. The address of the Chesa Grischuna happened to be Bahnhofstrasse 12, 7250 Klosters. A room at the Chesa is $238 per night. The General was totally surprised. The General got interested in the hotel, and asked the Storchen concierge if he could find the persons with reserved tables at the Chesa, but was told that information was not available.

After arriving in Klosters, the first thing that Anna said to the General was," I'd love to write a book on Klosters." The General and Anna had a glorious time. A luxury apartment was available for sale on the other side of the Bahnhofstrasse. The General asked the price, and it was agreeable. The General asked about residency and was told the buyer could only be a Swiss citizen or a person who could show they could support themselves. The General went out on a limb and made an offer on the apartment. While filling out the application for purchasing the apartment, the General mentioned that he was a retired four-star general in the U.S. Air Force, and the salesman said the application would be accepted forthwith. He said, "Switzerland is a military country and officers are encouraged to live here, regardless of their place of origin."

On the train ride back to Zürich, Anna said to the General, "You are a crazy guy to buy that apartment in Klosters. Are you going to propose to me?"

"That isn't my intention," said the General. "We're both wealthy and well-positioned. I'm not sure we need to."

Anna didn't say a word.

THE MATH CONFERENCE IN ZÜRICH

The math conference was a total success. The compliments floating around were centered on how well Americans can put on a conference. Most math publishing companies were there and paid a hefty price to display their books and attract authors. Several mathematical development companies were there to recruit employees. They also paid a large fee to the conference. For the first time, a large profit was made by the math conference – even though it was being held in a foreign country. The program chairman was a hero, and the phrase flowing around was *The business of America is business.*

Alexi's paper went well, and it was heard that he was a better speaker in English than most Americans. It was also heard that Russians are good at learning languages.

Matt's paper went well also, but the level of the subject matter was very high and the required math knowledge was unbelievable. Matt was, without question, the best mathematician in the world.

Alexi and Matt met after presenting their papers and congratulated each other. Matt recommended the Sprüngli restaurant on the Bahnhofstrasse for lunch. Bally Shoes fascinated Alexi, and Matt guessed that fashionable shoes were rare in Russia. Matt thought he should buy himself a pair before he left Switzerland.

The lunch at Sprüngli was exceedingly pleasant. Both men had potato soup and a roast beef sandwich. Alexi questioned what Matt did in his free time, and Matt said they were working on the COVID-19 virus problem and were at a standstill because of the diverse countries working on the subject. At present, there were three countries working on a vaccine: Russia, England, and the United States. It appeared as though each country was looking at a separate virus. Alexi was unusually quiet for a few minutes and then said, "Possibly, I can help."

"In what way?" Asked Matt.

"We have an outstanding virus biologist by the name of Dr. Dimitri Aplov, who might be interested in collaborating with an American scientist," said Alexi.

"What if the American scientist is a woman?" asked Matt.

"Some scientists in Russia are women," said Alexi. "It is true that most medical doctors that see patients are women, and most men are engineers, physicists, and mathematicians. However, in Russia, there is no concern over whether a scientist is a man or a woman. It is the result that the country is interested in."

Well, I might as well tell you," said Matt. "that the woman involved is my wife. Her name is Ashley Miller. She is quite intelligent and has a good knowledge of the problem domain."

"That doesn't matter," answered Alexi. "Many research teams in Russia have both men and women. However, if she visits Moscow State University, you must accompany her, because otherwise the authorities will think she is a spy. We have a spy mentality. You must hurry though, our common vacation schedule is in the near future."

"Okay, tell me when it would be convenient.," said Matt, "We will be there whenever it is convenient for Dr. Aplov."

"Plan on next week, and I will speak with him back in Russia," said Alexi. "I am returning to Russia tomorrow."

"Okay," said Matt. "Call me when you can. I will be here an additional day, as we will return to the States two days from now."

"I have one more thing to tell you," said Alexi. "Dr. Aplov would like to visit the United States for a year or more – especially, since I will be in residence there. Perhaps, even for a longer time."

The two men shook hands and parted. Both had a smile on his face."

The next day, Matt bought his Bally shoes and waited for the General and Anna to return to Zürich.

12

FLIGHT TO NEWARK INTERNATIONAL

The Flight from Zürich's Kloten Airport to Newark International took a little less than six hours. The pilots got the Gulfstream ready for the return trip without any difficulty. The General had a pleasant time and several good meals. Anna was a bit embarrassed, but thoroughly enjoyed herself. Matt was extremely tired and quiet. The General asked if things were okay, and Matt said they were, but he had a lot to think about. Once he got started, he had plenty to say.

"I have some things to report to the two of you, and another thing or two to think about," said Matt. "I talked to Harp, and he had some interesting results from the pandemic simulation runs. The expected results from the simulation runs did not match actual real life data. Also, the mathematician Alexi Belov will come to the States permanently. The Dean of Foreign Affairs and I have worked out the required procedures through the state departments of both countries. Oh, by the way, Kimberly, Harp's wife, is pregnant and is due any day now."

Neither companion said anything,

Matt continued. "My plan to use Alexi as a source for recruiting a virologist, which seemed rather obvious to me, turned out fine. He recommended an associate of his, Dr. Dimitri Alapov, who had expressed interest in coming to work with us for a short time with the possibility of a permanent position. It seemed a little too easy to me, but the Russians are a subtle kind of people. There is more to it. Remember, Ashley has planned on the eventuality of being a sort of pandemic expert and being the interface between us and the virology expert in Russia. Now I found out that she needs a male companion, because otherwise, the authorities will think she is a spy. So, I will have to accompany her, and I don't feel like doing it. I'm not sure I have the time. Also, flights from the U.S. are frowned upon. So we would have to fly to a safe location, such as Switzerland, and then fly to Russia on a Russian or Swiss airline. That is not a big challenge, but who wants to make a connecting flight. Actually, I'm more concerned over how much Ashley knows about the subject. Remember, I just mentioned that Alapov was interested in coming here. so that is another possibility. Perhaps, the interface with Alapov is not as important as I thought. There might be another option."

"Maybe I can help you somewhat," said the General. "As a former military general officer, I am sure that I can fly the Gulfstream into a Russian Army airbase. It has been done before. During World War II, we flew a B-29 into Russia.

But, of course, we were allies then. I think the military has a good memory, so maybe it will work."

All Matt could say was, "I think I am going to get a couple of books on immunology."

"I have another thought on the subject," added the General. "Remember, we are primarily interested in the source of the virus, and perhaps the subject is not as sophisticated as the CDC people seem to think it is. I have planned to visit Prince Michael, or Sir Michael, as they now call him, because he apparently has some unique ideas on the subject. Also, he might have some evidence. I think I will contact Buzz."

The General looked over at Matt, who was looking at Anna, and smiled. Things were getting complicated, and he liked that.

The long flight from Switzerland to New Jersey took a great circle route, so the flight time was a little shortened. It would be great to sleep in your own bed and eat some of your own food.

The General wondered how much of the information on the pandemic was actual fact, or was some kind of political fiction – yes, a political novel without truth, except in the imagination of the author.

PART II

FROM RUSSIA

13

HOME IN NEW JERSEY

Matt and Ashley were happy to see each other. She was lonesome, and he was kind of bored visiting Switzerland, even though it is possibly one of the best places – if not the best – on planet Earth to visit. The General was more joyful, as he would soon be the owner of an apartment across the street from the majestic Chesa Grischuna where he would probably have a *stom tische*, meaning a reserved table, when he was in the village. The General wondered how many of his meals he would eat there. He wondered if he should marry Anna before moving there, but could not make up his mind whether there was anything in it for him. He didn't like the fact that it seemed like every personal decision was handled like a business decision. Weren't some personal decisions made on an emotional basis?

The General wondered about flying into a military base in Russia. After the Nuremberg Accord, he knew plenty of Russian officers, and they were probably still active in the military in an advisory position. He decided to try, because of Matt's thoughts on the matter. He felt sorry for his grandson, who was getting into something he probably was not interested in, and probably knew very little about. He, himself, didn't care a whit about human immunology, and he thought Matt felt the same way on the subject.

The General felt sorry for Anna. She had ended her career and wanted something. Perhaps, he and she were in the same position in life.

The team had no one else except Buzz, who could help them out. Well, perhaps Amelia. She was in Ohio doing who knows what. Did the Russians in the virus research department know her? Could be they would not recognize her. Who would know? Perhaps the President should be consulted. Things were getting complicated.

The General called President Strong on his private line.

"Hello, Mr. President, this is General Miller."

"Well, how are you General? I've been thinking about you and your team. Have you heard the latest news?"

"Probably haven't," said the general. "We were in Switzerland on business of a sorts."

"Well, it is serious – very serious. They have discovered a mutation to COVID-19 in England," said the President. "I am worried, very worried about this country. After every holiday and practically every Saturday night, the country goes crazy again and the immunization rate hits the ceiling."

"You need help," said the General.

"I need help, and I need it in the form of you and your team," replied the President. "Can you and Matt and Ashley be here tomorrow.?"

"We can, but we might need more people to handle this situation," said the General. "Kimberly Harp is unavailable, and the German and English group is no longer appropriate, except for Prince Michael."

"How about Amelia?" asked the President. "She's probably tired of that university stuff by now."

We are going to visit the virus lab at Moscow State University with Ashley, but Amelia with her STEM background would perhaps be better," said the General. "On the other hand, the Russians might recognize her."

"Then have her work undercover, if they do." Said the President. "I'll have her here tomorrow afternoon. Can you and your team be here at 2 pm?"

"We can if you have more than one White House jet," replied the General.

"We now have three new jets and six pilots,: said the President. "We'll have you here at 2 pm. I have to go, I still have a job. It's the Security Council again. It seems I'm always talking to it."

"Okay, tomorrow then," said the General.

14

HOME BUT NOT FOR LONG

"Are you serious?" asked Matt. "We go to the White House tomorrow?"

"There is a mutation to the Pandemic virus," said the General. "The President is concerned."

"What time?" asked Matt.

"Two o'clock is the meeting," said the General. "Be ready with Ashley at 9 am. He's bringing up Amelia. I think this is a serious situation."

"Exactly, what happened?" asked Matt.

"They have discovered a COVID-19 mutation in England," said the General, "and the President thinks it will affect the nation. Be ready at 9 am. I'll pick you up."

"What's happening?" asked Matt.

"They have a lockdown in London, and people can't go out unless they have a valid reason."

Ashley was very glad to have Matt home. "Empty houses are lonely Matt," said Ashley. "I'm glad we have a light day tomorrow. I need a trip to Starbucks."

"So do I," replied Matt. "Something has come up. There is a mutation in the COVID-19 virus and the world is in big trouble. We have to be at the White House tomorrow at 2:00 pm. We leave at 9:00 am. You are the immunization expert and I think we are going to need you."

"Are you going, Matt?" asked Ashley. "I don't want to go alone."

"We go together with the General," explained Matt. "He will pick us up at 9:00. I know I already said this. We go to the airport and are picked up by one of those White House jets that is always running. It's like it was in our last trip. We'll be back for dinner."

"He better give us a Green Room dinner," said Ashley. "We deserve it."

"We do indeed," replied Matt. "Amelia will be there. The President likes her, I think, but he doesn't have anyone else to work with us on his problems – whatever they are. He has only Michael left in England besides Buzz. The two jokers from England and Germany are no longer available. By the way, Kimberly is pregnant and due this week. Naturally, Harp will be unavailable also. So, that's it."

"Those two guys didn't do much anyway," added Ashley. 'Buzz was correct by firing them."

"You're right there," said Matt. "It was instructive for them to be chewed out. They deserved it."

"Let's go to the Green Room by ourselves," said Ashley. "We need a change."

Matt and Ashley entered the Green Room. The General and Anna were already seated.

"Please join us," aid the General.

Ashley's heart sank. She so much wanted to be alone with Matt.

The General was in a good mood, a very good mood indeed. It was so inviting, when he was in a good mood, that he drew everyone into his world of pleasure. He liked action, and the upcoming job could be very interesting.

"I can't tell you when they are here," said Matt. "I'll tell you on the way home."

"Hi, Anna," said Ashley cheerfully. "Did you buy any shoes in Zürich?"

"I knew you would ask," answered Anna. "We didn't even pass the Bally store on the Bahnhofstrasse. How was your time in peace and quiet?"

"It wasn't that bad," answered Ashley. "I got a lot of my work done. We're running virtual courses at the college, and it's a big job setting things up. It was a little scary, though. When you are alone, you hear every little noise. But, I got used to it. Matt was gone too long. How was your trip to Switzerland?"

"Well, I have to say that your friend, the General, has purchased a residence in Klosters. It's really nice, and it comes with a reserved table at a classy restaurant named the Chesa Grischuna. Have you heard of it?' asked Anna. Hoping to get a one-up on Ashley.

"Of course," answered Ashley. "Everyone knows that it is the special restaurant of Deborah Kerr, the well known American actress."

Anna was clearly disappointed. Everyone knew that Ashley was a favorite of the General.

The dinner at the Green Room was typical. The General had filet, and the others had fish. No one was particularly hungry, and they left early.

"You were going to tell me something before dinner," said Ashley to Matt. "Do you remember what it was?"

"Of course," said Matt. "Have I ever forgotten anything, since you met me?"

"You forgot my birthday," said Ashley. "Just kidding."

"Most men work all of their life, probably 40 or 50 years. A lot of days are the same. Get up, get ready, have breakfast, battle the traffic, and start the workday. A guy can't get to work, and take a short nap. This will eventually happen to women, also. A lot of women get off after a long day, kick off those terrible shoes, and have a class of wine. Anyway, most men do that for more than a few years and then retire. It's hard to sit back and retire. That's why, I think, that men like the General are always go, go, go."

"They should play golf," replied Ashley. "I see your point. When they get up in the morning, they are used to go, go, go."

"That sounds humorous," said Matt. "But, I think it is probably true. Even I do my best thinking in the morning."

"I suppose all of that is true," said Ashley. "So when do we leave tomorrow morning?"

15

TO THE WHITE HOUSE AGAIN

When the team got to the local airport at 9:00 am the next day, the White House jet was already running. It was a new aircraft, and it had plenty of power for an unbelievably fast ascent. Someone, somewhere was in a hurry for something or another, a big hurry.

The jet got to Washington, D.C., and a Marine One was waiting. Its rotors were turning and several Marines were standing by the entrance. There were no decoy helicopters today. It was total business, and very serious business.

The team consisted of Matt, the General, and Ashley. No one knew what to expect in the White House. The General broke the ice by asking Ashley what she had come up with on the subject of the vaccine. Ashley was a little hesitant, and then she came out with following reply.

"I am sorry to say that there is very little written on the subject – at least, what I have access to. Neither the college nor the library had anything. But, I do have information from the Internet that could help us. A vaccine is an organism with spikes on the surface like a virus. Actually, it is a virus of a sort. A few spikes are inserted into a human immune system which creates antibodies to fight off the COVID-19 virus. The process is ingenious, but the manufacture and distribution of the so-called vaccine is complicated, as is the verification that the virus is okay for human use. So far, that's all I know. I suspect when a virus mutates, its characteristics change, and the older vaccines do not work with the new mutated virus. I suspect we are here to investigate the situation. It's complicated because we don't know where the mutated virus came from, and so forth. In fact, we know decidedly little about the total problem."

"That's very good," said the General. "Ashley, you are amazing."

So the team met in the President's private office to discuss the mutated virus.

16

THE WHITE HOUSE MEETING

The President was cordial, and the atmosphere didn't seem at all like there was a national crisis right around the corner. Amelia Robinson was there from her job in Ohio. Another White House jet brought her from a local airport in southern Ohio to Washington in the same way the rest of the team was retrieved from New Jersey.

When the team entered the President's private office, customary American hugs were exchanged. Amelia was particularly gracious – possibly relieved from the dull life of a university administrator.

"Hi everyone," said Amelia with a gigantic smile on her face. She was beautiful, tall, lean, and tanned. Her hair bounced around like it was guided from outer space. "I've really missed you."

"We missed you too, Amelia," said Ashley, who was caught up in the excitement. She and Amelia were good friends. They really liked each other.

Even the General was pleased. It was not usual for a General in the military to experience such pleasant behavior.

The President soon tired of the pleasantries and finally said, "Time to get down to business."

The President hesitated a few seconds, unsure if he should continue with his planned opening remarks. "To avoid any difficulties, let me say that we know what you folks have been up to. Amelia, we know you have been primarily in the Registrar's office. Ashley, you've been at the college. Les, you have been buying an apartment in Klosters, and we know about Deborah Kerr and her reserved table in the Chesa restaurant. That Swiss couple ahead of you on the train to Klosters were American with a directional mike. Now Matt, you were a definite challenge, since you appeared to spot the 3-letter boys from the U.S. who were tailing you. By that I am referring to the 3-letter agencies like the CIA."

"I did notice someone was tailing me. It has happened before. I believe I saw every one of them," said Matt with a sly smile on his face. "In my presentation, there was some guy in a brown suit and white socks furiously taking notes in a really advanced presentation. That would be impossible to do. He was also in the James Joyce, when I was talking to the program chairman, with a woman wearing a wire. Her head bounced every time I changed the decibel level. Then, walking down the Rennweg to the hotel Storchen in Zürich, I saw two men talking casually, trying to act as if they weren't looking at me. When I got even with them, they looked away, so as to protect their faces. After I passed, they headed in the other direction. Then at the Storchen Hotel, a person doing the trailing was waiting for me to end a visit with Harp and Kimberly, who are having a baby. Then he followed me on my subsequent walk to the James Joyce to visit with a famous Russian, who is going to come the States as a professor. I would like to assure you that we, at the university, have recruited a famous mathematician named Alexi Belov, and have done so to improve our math department. I also met with the program chairman from Stanford, but I saw no one on my tail at that time. Now you know the official story."

"You are in the wrong business, Matt," said the President.

"I don't think so," said Matt. "I have a good job, but I must admit that I have a unique ability to spot differences without actually looking for them, just like the new figurines on your desk. They look nice. You have changed them."

The President smiled at that and said, "You never know about people."

"Maybe we should get going on the subject of our visit," commented the General. "We have a time schedule," which wasn't true and everyone knew it. Military general officers are used to controlling a meeting.

The President couldn't get off the case of Matt, who saved the President's wife in an earlier case. She called Matt, Dr. Matt, her hero, because of his gentle manner.

"Matt, can you go over the process of recruiting a faculty member from a foreign country?" asked the President.

"We have a Dean of Foreign Relations, and he has worked it out with the state departments of the U.S. and Russia. It's a done deal," said Matt. "However, we plan to use him as an entry to the virology program in Russia to determine what's going on with the pandemic and the mutation. The Russian is named Dr. Dimitri Aplov, and he is the top-notch scientist in the world in that area. We feel he was the major contributor to the Russian vaccine that appears to have taken the world by surprise. The vaccine appears to work well. There is one more thing. Ashley has done an excellent job of bringing the team up to date on vaccines and immune systems. We expect her to participate in the Russia program. The General will be handling the vital information on the mutation in England, where it seems to have originated. His contacts there are more than substantial."

"I'm impressed," said the President. "I thought I had something totally new. In the President's Daily Brief, known as the PDB, it was reported as a small initial outbreak to which we are responding. I iniated this meeting, and now I'm playing a minor role. General, can you tell us how you plan to proceed?"

"Thank you, Mr. President," said the General. "The situation is different than we expected even though our expectations were actually ill-defined in the first place. Remember, I'm talking without explicit preparation, so please bear with me."

The General continued, "Here is the plan that I envision at this exact moment. It will probably change a little:

- We have to verify that the mutation is a serious threat to the U.S., and other nations.

- We need to somehow relate the threat to a source.

- We need to find out what other countries are doing about the threat, other than waiting for the U.S. to solve all of the world's problems.

- We have to look into the actions of England, Russia, and probably Germany – because they are good at vaccines.

- We have to alert the pharmaceutical industry as to the direction they should take.

Thank you."

"I know your team normally includes Matt, Ashley, and Mme, Purdoine, that you call Anna, and Amelia. Sir Bunday and Sir Michael seem to be supplementary. We are also interested in how the British Monarchy views the subject," said the President. "Amelia, you're the only person left, but we value your knowledge and especially your judgment, as much as anyones."

"I, like the others," said Amelia, "am not here with a plan. However, I have knowledge of the Russian and English systems."

"Wouldn't the Russian knowledge that you have be a distraction to your participation?" asked Matt.

"I don't think so," answered Amelia. "The spy program I was in is totally distinct from normal operations, and besides, they don't care. If you are not doing something for them, they forget about you. I have met Dimitri Aplov, but that was before I had my final face-lift. In addition, I am knowledgeable in practical virology, so there will be a person the Russians can communicate with."

"Okay, let's get out of here," said the President. "The General is in charge, and the operational procedures are the same as before. Let's try to have something in a few weeks. One more thing, Amelia, I know the President of your university, and we can work out anything that pleases you. I have heard, by the way, that he would like to have a high-level virology department at the university. If you would like to get out of the registrar position, we can work it out. Remember, the United States of America needs this, so be prudent."

"When do we start?" asked Ashley.

"You're started, Ashley," answered the President with a smile. "The White House jets are available to you at any time. Oh, General, I have a minor point that may turn out to be a major point. Our work on this project is **top secret**. The military in the person of Mark Clark, and the other agencies that we know so well are off limits. You will find the reason for this at a later date. Bon voyage."

The flight from Washington, D.C. to New Jersey was miserable. Amelia was uncomfortable not having been a member of the team for some time, and not knowing her exact role in the project. Ashley tried to comfort her, to no avail. Clearly she was not completely pleased with her university appointment in Ohio, but on the other hand, she wasn't exactly happy with the most important event in the nation's history either. Matt jumped in and attempted to ease the situation with Amelia. "Amelia, we understand your situation. Don't be concerned. We know you like to take charge of things. Ask Ashley what she thinks."

The General finally said, "If you want out of the project, Amelia, you may pull out now. We didn't choose you. The President did."

Matt wondered why some people were so tough on other people.

Amelia shaped up, and Matt, who was keenly observing the situation, was relieved. They had important work to do and needed good people.

17

HOME AGAIN

On the flight to New Jersey, Matt and the General sat together in the last row.

"Do you know that we are in the safest seats in the plane," said Matt. "If we crash, the plane usually splits just behind the wings. Above the wings is the most dangerous spot."

"My boy, do you think there is anything I don't know about flying and aircraft design?" answered the General.

"Just making small talk," said Matt. "By the way, why don't you pilot anymore?"

"I don't exactly know," replied the General. "It's like the marathon runner that has run more than 90 marathons and then experiences a knee injury and has to have his knee replaced. To that person, running is over and it's time to move on. So it is with my piloting. I do not feel like doing it anymore."

"Do we know anything about vaccines?" asked Matt. "There are a lot things that are just now coming into vogue, like a Theory of Everything and String Theory and the math of Black Holes," said Matt. "Vaccines and viruses are in the same domain. How about you? I know you read a lot."

"Same with me," replied the General. "I think it is time for your Ashley to take on a major role."

"Okay with me," said Matt. "She's a smart girl – I mean lady."

"How about a couple of rounds of golf, because when we get started with our new project, we might not have a lot of free time?" Asked the General."

"What about the next two or three mornings?" Asked Matt.

"Sounds good to me," answered the General, as the White House jet landed.

Matt whistled a tune as he drove to the Country Club. *You get out on the course,* he thought, *and you don't have a worry in the world.* Matt chose a set of new clubs acquired in a recent trip to Maui. They made him feel good. Funny thing, the General felt exactly the same way.

Out on the course, the weather was crisp, and both Matt and the General wore a fashionable golf jacket. On this day, Matt and the General were trying out a new kind of golf ball that spins faster. *That's the way sports are,* thought Matt. *Always something new.*

"I'm sorry to say this, Sir," said Matt. "I see we are being tailed."

"Well, I might have a new theory on that," replied the General. "Now listen carefully. Is it possible that they are tailing us for another reason than surveillance? We are remarkably successful and perhaps someone, namely the President, would like to know how we do it. We have a very good reputation."

"You may be right, of course, but that is certainly a strange way to do it," said Matt. "I'll keep my eyes open and see what happens."

The golf game was successful. The fast spinning balls seemed to make a big difference, as they break the air more sharply.

"Do you think we need a meeting?" said the General just after the ninth hole.

"I do think we need one, but I'll tell you that I don't exactly feel like having one. I wish I knew more about the immune system and pathogens," said Matt.

"We've got Amelia here," replied the General. "She can't just sit around forever."

"Okay," said Matt. "I guess you want me to make an agenda for all of us."

"I do," said the General. "Have you thought tonight at the Green Room at 6:00, special room, for a meeting. Of course, only if you can. I know it's a lot of work."

"I'll be at the dinner with Ashley," said Matt. "I'll let you bring Amelia and make a decision on your Klosters friend Mme. Purgoine, known as Anna."

"What do you want me to decide about them?" asked the General.

"That's up to you," said Matt. "Maybe you should call Sir Bunday," said Matt. "He may have some suggestions, and he has an in with Sir Michael."

"That's all we can do at this stage," said the General.

18

THE RUSSIA PLAN

The General called Buzz Bunday, now known as Sir Charles Bunday, after receiving his knighthood of the United Kingdom. Buzz answered on the first ring of his satellite phone.

"Bunday here," said Buzz. "Hope you're having a great day."

"I am and it's me, your old buddy," said the General. "How are you doing, Sir Charles?"

"Well, this Knighthood stuff is definitely not what it is played up to be," said Buzz. "I'm expected to make all these appearances and smile a lot. How are you doing old buddy? Did you read about UFOs in today's newspaper?"

"I've been a little busy this morning and did not see it," answered the General.

"Apparently, the CIA has released something like 10 thousand reports on UFOs," said Buzz. "I guess it was in response to a Freedom of Information Act request. Made me think of our experience. Do you remember?"

"Not exactly," said the General.

"It was when the new P-51s came in and you and I were given the honor of testing them out," said Buzz. "It was to help younger pilots use the capabilities of the new aircraft. It was fast and maneuverable and a big jump in capability. It was fast, and I remember you were trying to see if it could go the requested speed. You got up to 423, if I have the number right. You spotted a UFO, and we took out after it. It just sat there and then when it spotted us, it took off like a shot. When we landed, the CO was on our case for using so much fuel. We never told anyone, since we were afraid we would get grounded."

"Now I remember, I always wondered about something," said the General. "Why do UFOs always have their lights on? I thought we always flew with our lights off."

"I guess they want us to know they are there," said Buzz. "I'm sure that is not why you called."

"We have another project with the U.S. gov and could use your help," said the General. "As usual, it's high priority. It concerns the vaccine situation and the mutation situation. Our sponsor, and you can guess who it is, wants to be on top of it. So, it's **Top Secret.** The report in England of the mutation started the ball rolling. We don't know anything about it, and it might be a disaster. Essentially, our action will define the project. It will focus on the vaccine, mutation, or even something else."

"I know it well," said Buzz. "We are in total lockdown. Only, essential services are allowed on the streets. The King addressed the people, which he never does. You know the Queen retired and her private name is Kathleen Penelope Radford – I guess you already know that. Even she addressed the nation. My counterpart, Sir Prince Michael, who is a big deal around here, after conquering the vaccine, is leading a national investigation into the mutation. I have a question about this virus stuff, Les. Do you know anything about the virus and pandemic, like where did it start, why did it start, and what are all these scientists, receiving fantastic salaries, doing about It? Or, not doing about it."

"Well, Buzz, I would say we are in the same boat, and it appears to be sinking," replied the General. "All I've gotten involved with is a flu shot. I'm not exactly sure what a virus is and the whole subject is, at this moment, beyond me. I'm going to leave it to Matt, because he likes to know everything. He can have one of our staff, such as Ashley, look into it. But, I hasten to add that knowing all about these things does not solve our problem."

"You are a pilot and so am I," said Buzz. "That's good enough for me. I personally do not care much about these round viruses with spikes sticking out of them."

"I guess that this stuff is part of life," answered the General. "If a person doesn't know it, they are missing part of life."

"Okay, okay, I'll do whatever is necessary," replied Buzz. "It could be interesting."

"Make a contact with Sir Michael, and I'll let you know what we need to do. The honorarium is $200,000, so that will ease the pain."

"There is one other thing that you can perhaps do that might help us and the project. Bear with me for a couple of minutes. Matt has a famous mathematician coming to the U.S. for permanent residence. It's being handled by a Dean of Foreign Relations at the university, and the Secretaries of State in the United States and Russia. It's perfectly legal. We would like to bring out a famous virologist who invented the Russian vaccine. It is also perfectly legal and handled by the same people. Matt is going there for the pick up. That's the way it works. Using commercial airlines is more than cumbersome. Would it be possible to fly the Gulfstream into Russia and land at an old air base, possibly one that is not being used and just sitting there. I know that the Russian air force will escort the Gulfstream in with a fighter, but our boys are retired F-22 Raptor pilots. Fuel might be a problem, so we might have to stop in England for a refuel before we go in. I know how it works, because during the Nuremberg war trials, I flew a B-29 in. I can handle the local stuff like hotel and ground transportation. The professors there can help, since professors are like gods in Russia."

"Shouldn't be a problem," said Buzz. "I'll check with the guys I know in the British Air Force."

"Thanks, Buzz," said the General.

"Thank you. Les," replied Buzz. "You are a good buddy."

The General just sat there. He looked at a report by a U.S. doctor entitled, 'How Many Might Die Even With a COVID Vaccine?' in which the expected infection rate with the vaccine will be inexplicably high. It read that with the vaccines, the number of people who will contact COVID is estimated to be 77 million – in the U.S. alone. It was time for action.

The General called Matt, "Matt, would you like to go to Russia to pick up the mathematician Alexi Belov and hopefully the virologist Dimitri Aplov?"

"Is this an extraction or an ordinary business trip?" asked Matt.

"It is perfectly legal, and so forth," said the General. "Buzz is checking on it. I don't know how to arrange it, so Buzz is checking on it through the British Air Force. We are not at war, and militaries seem to be getting along. Anyway, put this Russian operation in your plan, and I'll let you know as soon as Buzz replies."

"Okay," said Matt. "See you this evening."

A minute after the conversation, the General's satellite phone rang. It was a call from Buzz in London.

"Miller here," said the General.

It's Buzz, I have good news for you and it wasn't even difficult. It's a common practice. Our air director can arrange it. You would be allowed to land at Kubinka air field in Moscow."

"That's where I landed the 29," snuck in the General.

"Once you enter Russian air space, you will be escorted by a Russian Sukhoi SU-57 fighter. The flight, for you, would be roughly 4,700 miles, and you probably can make it in 10 hours – they say 9 hours and 56 minutes. I'll find out about ground transportation, and I think you probably should ask your contact there to arrange it."

"That's good work, Buzz," said the General.

"There's more," said Buzz. "You can sympathize with me on this, as a pilot. I think you might want to refuel in London on your way in. That way you will be able to leave Moscow with more than enough fuel to get back to London or even the U.S. Refueling in Moscow probably won't be a problem, but you never know."

That is a good plan, Buzz," replied the General. "It's prudent to cover all of the possibilities."

"Otherwise, you are good to go," replied Buzz.

"Thanks Buzz, you're the best."

19

THE OPERATIONAL PLAN

On the way to the 6:00 pm meeting at the Green Room, Matt asked Ashley if she had anything to present or say and Ashley, always one step ahead of the crowd, said she did. It was a short piece about how the viruses spread, and how someone could become contagious, since she reasoned that the ultimate goal of the team was to investigate immunization. Perhaps, mutation could be covered later. She apologized that she hadn't done more, but the resource material she requested hadn't arrived yet. Matt said that anything she had developed was perfect, since no plan had been presented.

As the team walked through the dining area, a couple watched them intently. The woman said, I wonder what those people are doing. They look like the local PTA." Her companion looked at her in surprise. "I doubt it. Have you noticed the men have polished shoes, and the women are wearing dresses with high-heeled shoes. One of their cars is an expensive Tesla, and one of the others is a Porsche Taycan.

I would say we are in the company of very successful people. Perhaps, this is true of all Americans."

The General opened the meeting. "Greetings everyone," said the General. "We have a new project, supported by the President in his usual fashion, meaning your honorarium is substantial. The intelligence community warned him about the mutation that occurred recently and has since become aware that the major problem at this point – and I stress at this point – is the general problem of the vaccine. After a short meeting, we'll have the customary dinner."

"General," said Mme. Purgoine. "I actually do not know about viruses, vaccines, mutations, and all of the rest pertaining to the rest of that subject." She continued, "How many of the rest of you feel the same way?"

Everyone nodded, except Matt, who welcomed the challenge of learning about something relatively new. He strongly felt that if a subject was adequately presented, anyone who tried could be functional in that domain.

"It's time to get down to business," said Matt. "The General asked me to make a plan, and I have done so, and here it is."

Matt passed out a single sheet of paper, as follows:

PROJECT PLAN

Personnel

Project leader: General Miller
Technical staff: M. Miller, A. Miller, A. Robinson, M. Purgoine, Sir Bunday, Sir Michael

External support: International specialist
Basic research: Ashley Miller
International relations: Amelia Robinson
Documentation: Anna Purgoine
Methodology: Matt
Needs research: Matt, Amelia, the General,
International Specialist

Support

We need assistance on immunization,
pathogens, and vaccines and have selected
a Russian specialist. We will need him in
the States. Matt, the General, and Amelia
will make the arrangements. The method
will be for a Russian associate to make
the connection. We will travel to Moscow
to bring the associate on board and gain
assistance in some fashion from the Russian
scientist. Sir Charles Bunday will support
international travel and be the British
connection.

Operational Plan

In order to execute our assigned task, we need
appropriate information. We would like to
obtain the Russian scientist as an academic
scholar.

We plan to provide the following information to our sponsor:

Where did the virus come from?
Who is the developer?
How to handle mutations?
Are the mutations a national problem?

"To continue, we will discuss all of the above in order to approach the problem systematically," continued Matt. "Ashley has a short piece to get us started. How do you want to proceed, Ashley?"

"I'll pass out copies and simply present it," said Ashley. "It's rather short, but it is where we stand, so to speak, on the subject."

ASHLEY'S INTRODUCTORY SHORT PIECE

A virus spreads through the movement of persons in a social group or across state lines. Since the affected persons are most contagious a few days before he or she shows symptoms, it is convenient for someone who has not followed precautionary procedures to pass it to others without knowing it, and the contagious person passes it on in a similar fashion. Most persons do not realize that the COVID-19 virus is highly contagious and is easily transmitted between individuals. Countries like Italy and New Zealand that use strict contact tracing limit the spread of the virus and are considered highly successful.

The tension in the room was high. The special dinner, arranged by the General, quieted things down, and the meeting was considered an excellent way to initiate a project.

After the meeting, the General took Matt aside. Ashley, Amelia, and Anna went with them. He had to speak with them in an informal setting, not in a structured meeting.

"As you folks know," said the General. "We have some business in Russia. The primary reason we are going is to bring back to the states Matt's mathematical colleague Alexi Belov, and all of the necessary permissions have been worked out between the state departments of the Russian Federation and United States. It probably wasn't totally necessary, but the university administration wanted to be sure it is a clean move. The travel preparations have been made. We will take the Gulfstream, refuel in London for precautionary reasons, and land at Kubinka military air base in Moscow. We will make a hotel reservation at the Courtyard by Marriott Moscow. It is located at Voznesenskiy Pereulok 7 in Moscow We have no access to transportation facilities, so we are going to have to ask Matt's associate Alexi Belov for assistance in this regard. Matt will have to make arrangements for the Moscow itinerary with Alexi, and we will finalize our travel when the plans have been completed. I would guess that we will leave for Moscow in 3 to 7 days and spend 3 days in

Moscow, and then return to the U.S. We will probably be escorted in Russian airspace by a SU-57 fighter plane, which is the best the Russians have. Americans always get the most strenuous attention. My expectations are to return with Alexi and Dimitri. We will land in London at a military base for refueling and then fly on to New Jersey. We are fortunate to have to have Sir Bunday for assistance. On the other hand, his honorarium is quite substantial."

"Is that all we have to cover," asked Ashley. "We need a break."

"Not quite," responded the General. "Between now and them, we are going to determine what, when, and where we are going to use their expertise. Now, I'm finished."

"Can we stop a minute?" asked Amelia. "What am I supposed to be doing? What is my function?"

"Because of your Russian background, your job is to entice this Dimitri fellow to come to the U.S., either temporarily or for the rest of his career, as a resident," said the General. "We have to consult with the President about this, but I think this is how we could and should proceed. Matt, you are the point man in this operation."

On the way home, both Ashley and Amelia fell asleep. At home the General had a double scotch, and Matt just fell into bed for a good night's sleep.

THE MOSCOW TRIP

The next morning, Matt awakened at 6:30 and called Alexi Belov at the Moscow State University, before Matt had even had his first cup of coffee.

"Alexi, this is Matt Miller," said Matt.

"Hello Matt, I was hoping you would call today," said Alexi. "When can I come to the U.S.? All of the paperwork has been completed."

"We will fly to Moscow this week to pick you up and bring you to the United States of America. We will leave tomorrow and arrive the next day early in the morning, because of the time change. We will stay in Moscow that night at the Courtyard Hotel by Marriott Moscow and have a nice dinner at the Café Pushkin. We will return to the States the next day, and you will be with us."

"I am very happy to hear that," said Alexi. "I can help you in Moscow in any way you wish. I am totally free."

"I do have a special request," said Matt. "As you know, we have the pandemic situation in the States, and we have several people who feel that they need to meet with your international virus expert, Dimitri Aplov. They asked if I could arrange a short meeting with him. This has absolutely nothing to do with your travel to the States with me, and it will take only a few minutes. Our schedule – that is, yours and mine – will not be interrupted."

"Of course," replied Al. "I know Dimitri well and will arrange a meeting in the afternoon on the day you arrive. He has been telling me how fortunate I am and wishes that he could go to the States with me. I told him he has to write papers, lots of papers, so the Americans know about him. He has very good English, better than I, but says his writing in English is not so good. I told him his writing is good enough and better than most British people. I don't know about Americans."

"The meeting with Dimitri should take only a few minutes," added Matt. "If they are making good progress, then it might take a couple of hours, but no more. That is why we are staying in Moscow for the night. I will not go to that meeting unless I have to."

"You must go with them if they are women," replied Al, "otherwise the Russians will think they are spies."

"Okay, I will go then," said Matt. "But, I still want to spend a little time with you discussing string theory. Maybe after their meeting."

"I will be available," said Al. "Tell me where you will arrive. I will pick you up in a Russian limo that belongs to the university. It's not exactly a limo. They are being nice to me. They are hoping I will change my mind. I said, 'Never in a million years.'"

"We will travel in our special Gulfstream airplane," said Matt, "and arrive at the Kubinski military air base. I forgot one thing. Our leader, the General, has made a hotel reservation for you. You may accompany us if you choose."

"I will take you up on that," replied Al.

"Our landing permission at Kubinski was arranged in London through the English military attaché. Our group will contain four people: the General, myself, my wife Ashley, and a technical expert. We have plans to return with six, if everything works out."

Matt smiled. *Alexi did not pick up the subtlety in the return of six.*

"What should I bring with me?" Alexi asked.

"You should bring anything you please, especially your math books, and the university will arrange for the shipment of the remainder." said Matt. "Remember, this is a clean operation, which means that everything is legal and above board. If Dimitri wants to come to the U.S. with us, then the legal preparation has already been made."

"That is why the return number is six," said Alexi.

Matt smiled and nodded his head. Alexi did the same.

"Don't worry," added Matt. "If Dimitri agrees to come to the U.S., then everything is already arranged. Your housing has been assigned, and it is excellent. Something for Dimitri has already been planned. Remember, we will arrive in Moscow three days from now and I will confirm the expected time of arrival."

"Thank you, Matt." said Alexi. "I will prepare for the meeting with Dimitri, as you requested."

"Good bye, and I am looking forward to having you as a collogue of mine in the United States of America.," said Matt.

Matt had a quick breakfast with Ashley, who was beginning to regret the whole project. He headed to the university and an impromptu meeting with the Dean of Foreign Relations. The Dean gave Matt a look of hope and said he would have the associate at the state department take care of the situation.

"This operation involving Dimitri Aplov involves entry and residence in the country, and not an expenditure of the university for residence and employment," said the Dean. "By the way, have you secured your travel arrangements?"

"Yes, Sir," said Matt. "My grandfather, the General, is taking care of it." Matt thought it wasn't necessary to mention that the U.S. government was actually paying for it, in addition to a generous honorarium.

"Okay Matt," said the Dean. "You're a respected faculty member, and I will go along with your extracurricular activities. Good luck."

Matt called the General forthwith. "Everything is arranged, Sir," said Matt proudly. "By the way, good morning."

"Thanks Matt," replied the General. "I've been up since 6:30."

"Let me sum it up," said Matt. "We will meet with the virus expert on the afternoon we arrive. Depending on how things go, we should be able to leave Moscow the next day."

"What's going on with our knowledge of pathogenic viruses?" asked the General.

"Ashley got her books, so we will have to make a quick read."

"Okay then," said the General. "We leave in two days, and get there in three days."

"Are the travel arrangements all set?" asked Matt.

"No, not yet," answered the General. "We will stay at the Courtyard by Marriott Moscow. I don't understand the name, but that is another thing. The pilots and the Gulfstream have been taken care of. I'll do the flight plan this morning. I'll inform Amelia, and you should inform Ashley. I think that Amelia is a key person in the recruitment of the virus expert."

"Seems like she is," said Matt. "I was wondering if you were free for a quick 18 holes?"

"I am free," said the General. "I'll pick you up at your home in an hour."

"I'll be ready," said Matt.

21

PATHOGENS REPORT

When Matt returned from his round of golf with the General, Ashley was not too happy. She had been pouring over a book on viruses. Matt was totally amazed. Ashley had totally immersed herself in the study of viruses and related subjects. Matt looked at her papers, and the first thing she did was to make a meaningful outline, not the kind a student would make. Here is what it looked like:

Introduction and overview
What is a virus?
How a virus spreads
UK coronavirus variant
How do COVID-19 vaccines work.
Unfortunate destinations: movie theatres, bars, and mass transit
Herd immunity, present and future
Operation warp speed: delivery of the vaccines

Side effects of the vaccines
Distribution costs
The vaccine: how it works
Vaccine storage
mRNA: Pfizer and Moderna
Origin of viruses
Activities in China
Activities in Russia
Allergic reaction to vaccines
Miscellaneous comments

For Matt, Ashley had covered what they needed to know when they met with Dr. Dimitri Aplov. Apparently, Ashley's objective was to exhibit knowledge of the subject matter, but not too much. Otherwise, why call in a specialist.

The next thing that Ashley did was to consult with Amelia about Dimitri. She wanted an assessment of his character, and whether he liked educated women. Amelia knew about him as he had been the science associate when she was in training as a foreign officer. This led Ashley to ask if it was possible that Dimitri would recognize Amelia. Amelia responded that she had only one encounter with Dimitri and it was in a group meeting. Amelia received a face-lift before she was deployed to the United States and doubted that Dimitri would recognize her. Also, she would be speaking English, which was a little difficult for Russians, who were better at English speaking.

Ashley and Amelia discussed turning on the charm for Dimitri, and Amelia said she doubted it would help very much. There were plenty of good-looking women in Russia.

She said he would be more interested in what the possible position in the States would be like.

They discussed several possibilities, and finally Amelia hit on a winner, at least they thought so. Amelia had heard through her associates at the University in Ohio that the President of the University knew the President of the United States quite well. The University president also seemed to be quite aggressive and wanted to bring new programs or new research laboratories to the university. What about a virology research center funded by the U.S. government, which was regarded in Russia as a very rich entity?

Ashley and Amelia laughed over the idea, and finally Ashley said she could sell the General on the concept. They would bring it up on the flight to Moscow.

Ashley returned home after her brief meeting with Amelia, and really hit the books. She had good word processing skills, so she could enter information into a report as she studied the subject matter. Here is what she came up with.

COVID-19 REPORT

Introduction and overview. The literature on viruses states that there is no evidence that viruses came from extraterrestrials, or anything of the sort. Viruses occur through evolution and arose through various forms of cell activity. There is no known benefit of virus activity. Viruses attack a human cell and then exit that cell to live in another cell, a process known as replication. If a virus does not have another cell to invade, then it dies. This is what the literature says about the subject.

What is a virus? All living organisms contain viruses, and it has been estimated that the number of individual virus particles is 10 to the 31st power. That is a lot of virus particles, and many of them are not even alive. A virus is a parasite and lives off of a living cell. When it is out and about, it is inert, and if it doesn't find a cell to sponge off of, it dies. That is the basis of the various preventative measures, such as social distancing, masks, and washing hands. There is a thing called the R factor. If R=1, then each virus particle reproduces into one living particle. If R is less that 1, then more die than can reproduce and the virus dies. That is called the *herd immunity.* If R is greater than 1, then that is an epidemic. A virus has a shell, called an *envelope.* It is a protection for the particle. The envelope is a greasy membrane that protects the virus. Soap and water disrupts the greasy membrane and the virus dies. That is why washing your hands is so effective against the spread of a virus. A virus enters a cell and reproduces with an enzyme known as a *polymerase.* It reproduces and then moves to other cells. It is much more complicated, but that is the general idea.

How a virus spreads. A virus spreads from person to person through droplets that escape when you cough or sneeze. The droplets are emitted from a sick person and enter the mouths and noses of nearby people.

UK coronavirus variant. A variant is a mutation of a virus spore that is protected by a spike-like protection on its envelope. Whereas a virus is sensitive to heat, cold, and humidity, the protective spikes cause the virus to be more stable, but still sensitive to modern vaccines.

How do COVID-19 vaccines work. This type of vaccine uses a molecule named RNA to generate an immune response to a virus pathogen. The RNA teaches the cells to make an immune response.

Unfortunate destinations. Social distancing has forced sever types of businesses to shutter because of an inability to pay employees because of reduced revenue. The four most prevalent of this type of business are movie theatres, bars, restaurants, and all forms of live entertainment. Sports teams have been required to play without fans in the stands, such as in the case of football and basketball, and others to shut down completely.

Herd immunity. One of the major defenses against a pandemic is herd immunity. Herd immunity occurs when enough people are immune to a disease making the spread of the disease less likely. Usually, herd immunity is achieved through vaccination. What herd immunity means is that the spread of the disease from person to person is reduced.

Operation warp speed. The operation warp speed is a partnership between drug manufacturers to produce and distribute COVID-19 vaccines to 300 million Americans.

Side effects of the vaccines. The most common side effects of being given the COVID-19 vaccine are:

Pain, swelling, or redness at the point of injection
Mild fever
Chills
Tiredness
Headache
Muscle and joint aches

Many persons have no side effects. Each vaccine has unique percentages that experience the various side effects.

Distribution costs. Vaccines are purchased with U.S. dollars and distributed to the American people at no cost. The U.S. Congress has allocated $10 billion dollars for the solution to the COVID-19 pandemic.

How the vaccine works. The process that provides the vaccine, is exceedingly complicated. In the current version of a vaccine, the vaccine employs RNA strands that cause the immune system to attack and destroy the virus. No strands of the virus are included with the vaccine.

Vaccine storage. There are three manufacturers of COVID-19 vaccines: Pfizer, Moderna, and Oxford-AstraZeneca. Pfizer's and Moderna's vaccines must be kept in ultra cold storage. The Pfizer vaccine must be stored at -112 to -76 degrees Fahrenheit, the Moderna vaccine must be stored at -13 to -5 degrees Fahrenheit, and the Oxford-AstraZeneca at 36 to 46 degrees Fahrenheit.

mRNA: Pfizer and Moderna. The mRNA type of vaccine is a new method for making vaccines and uses non-invasive techniques.

Origin of viruses. This is a controversial topic in virus research. Most American virologists believe that viruses are inherent to the human condition and established through evolution. Many European researchers feel the source of viruses is created by man or inherited from extraterrestrial sources.

Activities in China. China has been blamed for the COVID-19 virus, because the original viral sequence occurred in Wuhan, China. The reason is that the virus is found in bats and Chinese people eat bats. This is likely untrue. China has not come up with a vaccine, but it has been an active participant in the WHO (World Health Organization.}

Activities in Russia. Russia has not been active in world affairs in the areas of viral and vaccine technology. The Russian country has announced they have developed a vaccine for COVID-19.

Allergic reaction to vaccines. Allergic reactions to COVID-19 vaccines are rare, measuring approximately 11 cases per million doses. The most prevalent reaction is *anaphylaxis* with onset approximately 3 hours after vaccination. Treatment for anaphylaxis is available, and patients are discharged shortly after being vaccinated.

Miscellaneous comments. One of the vexing problem in the COVID-19 pandemic is "How is it that the virus has spread so rapidly throughout the world." Outbreaks have surfaced at approximately the same time in remote locations. This fact has attracted attention in many areas.

END OF REPORT

Matt came home as Ashley was finishing up her work. He was amazed at what she had accomplished.

"Ashley, you are a wonder having finished the job so quickly. Did you know all of this virus information beforehand?" asked Matt. "It seems impossible to accomplish what you have in one day."

"I just filled in the report from the outline," answered Ashley. "I'm experienced at doing Internet research along with reference books."

"Well, thank you," said Matt. "I'm sure the General will be impressed. The knowledge gained from your report will surely help us with the Russians."

Matt called the General and had a quick message, "Sir, we're ready at this end. I should say that Ashley has finished her work"

"Thanks, Matt," said the General. "You two are a good team."

22

TO RUSSIA

The team consisting of Matt, the General, Ashley, and Amelia rode in the White House jet to Langley, where the Gulfstream had been moved in preparation for the flight to Russia. The pilot and co-pilot were ready to go, and the team was nervous, in spite of its high level of international experience. All they could think of was all of the things that could happen. Sir Charles Bunday had done a masterful job of lining things up. They would land at a British military air base for topping off the fuel tanks and then off to Kubinka air base in Moscow. Matt had called Alexi to relay their expected time of arrival. During the flight, Matt called him again and gave the actual time. Over the Atlantic, the pilots flew the Gulfstream at 600 miles per hour at 60,000 feet. When they entered Russian airspace, they slowed to 400 miles per hour and 40,000 feet. They were escorted, as expected, by a SU-57 fighter jet.

On the flight, Ashley gave Matt, the General, and Amelia a copy of her report. The General was impressed that she had done the complete job in a single day. Matt just smiled.

The team discussed their planned agenda: land at the Kubinka airfield, go through Russian border control, meet Alexi, probably have lunch at a restaurant of Alexi's choice, have Alexi drive Matt, Ashley, and Amelia to the university, discuss Dimitri's future, have dinner at the Café Pushkin, and stay oversight at the Courtyard Hotel by Marriott Moscow. In the morning, load the Gulfstream with Matt, the General, Ashley, Amelia, Alexi, and possibly Dimitri, load the plane with personal goods, and head on home. If there were no problems, they would be at Langley in 6 hours or so, and finally the White House jet to New Jersey. Amelia, Alexi, and Dimitri would stay at the General's home. The next morning, a few decisions and some communications had to be made, and then back to normal, if there was a normal in the General's life.

The General was primarily interested in Ashley's and Amelia's plan of operations. They would meet with Dimitri, exchange information on virology and vaccines, and then inquire about his future. Amelia would make mention of a lab at the university in Ohio, with the primary objective of finding what Dimitri thought about a Virology Research Lab at the university. The General picked up on the idea, as if it were his idea, and Ashley, Amelia, and Matt just smiled at their success.

Then, as if by plan, the General spoke of informing the President of the United States in such a way that he would adopt the concept as his own, and then have him play the same game with the President of the university.

"It's a great idea," said the General. "We have nothing to lose, and the government of the U.S. is paying us to do something that makes a difference in the area of the pandemic. Dr. Dimitri Aplov's expenses would be paid under the agreement they had made with the President. It was a win/win situation for them.

"Sir, what will you be doing," asked Matt, "when we are assessing the situation with Dimitri?"

"Thanks for asking," said the General. "I'm proud to inform you that I have contacted a Russian army general that I worked with on the Nuremberg war trials, and he proposed that we spend the day together. He had several ideas, so I left the afternoon up to him. I invited him to have dinner with us at the Café Pushkin restaurant that evening."

The flight was dull as dirt, and everyone dozed off, except Matt, who was studying a paper on mathematical string theory. There was always something new in the world of mathematics.

The fueling operation in England went as planned, as did the escort by the SU-57, Russian's competition to the American F-22 Raptor.

The landing at Kubinka military air base was quite a surprise to the Americans. They egressed from the plane and simply walked directly to the gate. There were no guards and no military. The pilots parked the Gulfstream and met up with the others at the gate.

Then they were hit with the second surprise. Alexi pulled up in a Checker Cab made in the U.S. in the 1970s. It was black and in practically new condition. Alexi said the Checker was owned by the university and was available for general use. The Russian General arrived in an almost new Cadillac sedan. Matt, Ashley, and Amelia got into the Checker, and the General and the two pilots got into the Cadillac. The only words spoken were by the General, "Meet you at the Café Pushkin when you are finished this evening."

The Russian General left the pilots off at the shopping area in Moscow, and the

American and Russian Generals headed for the countryside. As usual, the General was prepared. Each person on his team was given $1,000 in hundreds and twenties from the team's expense account. All the General said was, "The Russians like American currency. Enjoy yourselves."

The two generals headed to a countryside restaurant, for talking and dining. The pilots started walking to see what Moscow was like. The scholars headed to Moscow State University. Alexi parked the Checker Cab in front of the Virology Building, and the group headed inside.

23

DR. DIMITRI APLOV

"I will introduce the two women to Dimitri, and then Matt and I are headed out for some lunch," said Alexi. "We will be back soon."

Dimitri was cordial. He showed Ashley and Amelia his laboratory and explained what he was doing, which was vaccine development.

"We developed a vaccine here," said Dimitri. "We used the mBNA technique, and it works just fine. We don't do testing, like you Americans, but have results for actual patients. We are a little better than Pfizer and Moderna at 98%. Our allergenic reaction was and is zero. We have had no cases, so far. I'm referring to anaphylaxis. We do have epinephrine and anaphylaxis EpiPen available for treatment, but haven't had to use it thus far."

"You pronounce those terms perfectly," said Amelia. "Are you trained as a medical doctor?"

"I am one and also have a PhD in virology," replied Dimitri. "In Russia, only female doctors see patients. Men engage in research."

Amelia planned to address Dimitri directly about coming to the United States, as Russian men preferred straight talk rather than a lot of verbal fluff.

"Dr. Aplov, would you like to come to the United States to continue your research?" said Amelia. "We are prepared to offer you either a full-time position or a temporary one."

Dimitri was taken aback by Amelia's direct approach. Russian women were not that direct and forceful. Amelia was experienced in dealing with men with several large projects under her belt. For her, this was routine.

"I would prefer full-time, but what can you offer me about the position?" asked Dimitri.

"I can offer you a position as Director of a Virus Lab at a major university," replied Amelia. "You will directly oversee the development of the facility and the selection of personnel, as well as your routine research work. Your salary will be one hundred and fifty American dollars per year, plus free housing and a personal car."

Dimitri looked away.

"I can raise your salary to $200,000 if you request it," said Amelia. "Your position will be guaranteed by the President of the United States and your lab and operations will be administered by the President of the university. You will report to him and only him."

"When is this position available?" asked Dimitri.

"It is available immediately," answered Amelia. "You can come to the States with your friend Alexi, or you may come at a later time. If you come with Alexi, you will be given citizenship when you enter the country. No waiting. Alexi leaves for the United States of America tomorrow."

"Can I come with him?" asked Dimitri.

"You can do just that," replied Amelia. "We have a large modern airplane, called the Gulfstream 650, and you may bring as much as you please in reference material and personal items."

"Is that what Alexi is doing?" asked Dimitri.

"Yes, it I,." said Amelia. "He will work at the university in New Jersey with Dr. Matthew Miller. You will eventually work in the State of Ohio. That is where I work. It is beautiful."

"I will join you tomorrow," said Dimitri. "Thank you."

Dimitri looked at Amelia. She spoke like an American, and she had the honesty of a Russian, *This could be good, he thought.*

Matt and Alexi returned, and Dimitri gave them the news. They headed to a coffee shop to make a plan for the next day. Dimitri asked Alexi what he was going to bring on the travel to the U.S. Alexi responded that he would bring books and personal items. Other things would be shipped via commercial transport. Ashley gave the obvious solution. Ship all of his possessions, and have a friend or family member handle the transport. Dimitri said he lived at home, and he could ask his father to handle the shipment. His father had always wanted him to move to the U.S., where his talents would be more recognized, and would be pleased to handle the packing operation. The only concern for both Alexi and Dimitri was the move operation in detail, and Matt assured him that the state department of Russia and the United States would handle it. Matt looked over to Ashley, and she gave him the telltale look, *You'd better hope it gets done.*

The dinner at the Café Pushkin was a tremendous success, especially when the General paid for the evening in U.S. currency.

Neither of the two generals said anything during the entire evening. General Vladimir Gladair of Russia and General Les Miller of the U.S. said nothing about where they went and what they talked about during the entire afternoon. Later, Ashley asked Matt, who said they probably discussed military strategy. He added that there probably were few secrets at the military level.

It was strange," said Ashley. "All of us except for the generals drank coca cola at dinner, and the generals drank vodka and scotch."

"It is all in what a person is used to," said Matt. "I doubt that the Russians were copying the Americans."

24

THE FLIGHT HOME

The five passengers, along with the pilots, and their drivers met at the gate of Kubinka air base. Amelia and Matt were seen discussing the lack of security. Ashley overheard them and said it was probably no longer used. *The simplest solution was often the best,* thought Matt.

The Russians, Alexi and Dimitri, were more than pleased with the Gulfstream 650. It had been impossible to be refueled in Russia, so the pilots had to land in England. Sir Charles Bunday, as usual, was impeccable in his planning, and the refueling operation by the British Air Force was performed without incident. The landing in Langley was as smooth as silk, and the White House jet was waiting for them, and in relatively no time the group landed in New Jersey. The General's limo was waiting and shortly later, they were all relaxing in American luxury in the General's mansion. It was home to everyone, and that was the place to be.

Before they settled down for the evening, the General asked if Matt, Ashley, Amelia, and of course, himself could meet the next morning for a strategy meeting at Matt's home. Matt agreed and promised a special breakfast. Knowing Matt, they thought it would be a Matt special that consisted of yogurt, a scone, and coffee.

At the meeting, the team was totally surprised. They arrived at Matt's home expecting the yogurt special. Instead, they received a dozen assorted donuts, a dozen glazed donuts, and a Box O' Joe from Dunkin". Ashley was in on the deal, but the General, Amelia, a last minute guest in the form of Mme. Marguerite Purgoine, known as Anna, and the two Russian scholars new to America had no knowledge of what to expect. Even Matt, who had spent most of his life eating in a healthy way admitted that the breakfast was perfect for the occasion. It was good old American food.

Before, during, and after eating, the General repeatedly brought up the subject of the current meeting, which was that they had successfully recruited a renowned virus scholar and had a glimpse of the field of study in the report by Ashley, but what was next?

"We have only opened the door," said Matt. "We have not answered the how, what, why, who, and when for the question of the pandemic, the greatest incident to befall the U.S. and the rest of the free world."

"I agree, replied Amelia. "Don't we have some information from Sir Charles and the basis for a complete write up of what we have accomplished? It isn't much. Hopefully, our literary genius Anna will do that for us."

"What do you think, Anna?" asked the General.

"It would be my pleasure," said Anna. "I will consult with each of you and write a project report. Thank you for asking me to be a member of your distinguished team."

"Well, that's it then," said the General. "What's next for our newly appointed faculty, namely Alexi and Dimitri?"

"I can and will take care of Dimitri," said Amelia. "Can we arrange for the White House jet to take us to Ohio?"

"You can do it, but wait until I call the President of the U.S.," said the General. "I will call and fill him in. Then, I expect him to contact the President of the university, and we will be up and running. Most of the needs of all parties involved have been expressed previously.

"By the way," continued the General. "All of you, including our new colleagues, are invited to Klosters, before we get too busy again. This invitation includes Alexi and Dimitri. I have a few things to take care of in Klosters, and there is no sense in doing them alone. We can all take the Gulfstream to Kloten airport in Zürich, and then a train to Klosters. It's a nice place. We can spend a couple of days sightseeing, have some wonderful meals, do a little cross country skiing, and then return home. Afterwards, we can use it as a get-away or as a base for skiing. Who knows about the future. I wanted to come here before Amelia and Dimitri get too busy in Ohio. As for right now, I am going to call Sir Charles and then the President to let everyone know the schedule of events."

The General drove Amelia and Anna back to his mansion. Alexi and Dimitri were relaxing after a luxurious American breakfast. They agreed that the U.S. was definitely the place to live.

Amelia sat down with the Russians while the General went to his study to call Buzz Bunday, known politely as Sir Charles, and then to the President of the United States.

25

FINAL ARRANGEMENTS

The General called Sir Charles Bunday on his satellite phone. Sir Charles Bunday was called 'Buzz' by the General. They were war buddies, P-51 pilots that flew together. Buzz answered on the first ring.

"Buzz, how are you doing?" asked the General.

"I'm doing quite well, Les," said Buzz. "I heard you are back in the States. How was your trip to Russia, and was it successful?"

"Everything went as we planned it," replied the General. "Thanks for setting things up in England and in Moscow. We recruited the Russian scientist, and he is sitting downstairs. I'm at home. We have one more lead to follow, and then we are finished. We had good results. Have you had an opportunity to visit Sir Michael?"

"I have," said Buzz. "He was quite cordial, and we had a very useful conversation. When you are ready, I will summarize our conversation."

"I'm ready, Buzz," said the General.

"There is essentially nothing new," replied Buzz. "The mutation is scary since the new virus propagates so quickly. However, the vaccines are effective against it. He thinks the American vaccine is superior to the English one, but they all work satisfactorily. Because the virus spreads in multiple locations at the same time, he thinks it is airborne. He is convinced of that. As before, he says it is from Sahara wind or another galaxy. He says he has substantial evidence that it is extraterrestrial. The English media are always chasing one fancy or another, so I asked if it could be a plot to kill off people and save the planet. He was quite surprised that I asked about that. There has been a minor allergic reaction to the vaccine. Actually, it is not so minor. It kills the patient in fifteen minutes unless either of two medicines is administered. He says it is not a big worry, and it occurs only about eleven times in a million vaccinations. He says it might be caused by an underlying medical condition. In short, we are in the same position as we were before."

"Thanks, Buzz," said the general. "I'm going to contact the President, and 'call in' so to speak. I'll give him the option of initiating a virology center under his control. He has more than enough discretionary funds, since it in one of his budget line items."

The General called the President on his private line and got the secretary. He was told the President was in an important meeting. Ten minutes later, the President called back.

"Hi Les, what's going on?" asked the President. "I sincerely hope you have good results for me. That's what my meeting was about. It has turned into an important item."

"We do have a solution, Mr. President," replied the General. "I think you will be pleased with it."

"Go ahead, Les," answered the President.

"We have recruited the most prominent Virologist in the free world," continued the General. "He is an expert in all the areas you stressed, and more than familiar with practically every event that has occurred in the area of vaccines. He would be appropriate to develop a research center in a place or university of your choice."

"What about Ohio?" asked the President. "I know the president at the university and he is looking for a new program.

"Ohio would be ideal, and you have person there that could assist in the development of the program," replied the General.

"Do you mean Amelia Robinson?" asked the President. "She has a PhD for her work in Russia, but practically no one knows it."

"I knew it," replied the General.

"She developed appropriate software and cleaned up the Registrar's office," said the President.

"She's right here," said the General. "Would you like me to send her up along with Dr. Dimitri Aplov, the scientist from Russia. He developed the Russian vaccine."

"That would be a good idea before I contact the university President," said the President. "I'll send the White House jet for a pick-up in an hour and a half. They'll be back before dinner."

"Okay, Mr. President," replied the General. "They will be there."

In an hour and a half, Amelia Robinson and Dimitri Aplov boarded a White House jet to Washington and the White House. Amelia was pleased and cheerful. Dimitri was nervous and apprehensive.

At 3:00, the President called the General. "Les, it's all set up. The University President went for it, and I have used up some of my discretionary budget. Amelia and Dimitri are headed to New Jersey in a White House jet. Send me a final report and your project is complete. Residual expenses will be accepted as well as honorariums. Again, thank you."

The General gave the news to Matt, Ashley, Anna, and Alexi, and everyone appeared to be pleased. The team was tired. All Ashley wanted to do was sleep. Anna wanted to get started with her report. Matt and the General played a round of golf.

26

THE FINAL REPORT

"Les, I'm more than concerned over my final paper on the project and for the President," said Anna. "I have covered everything that is relevant to the problem, and it has been included in previous reports. Most of them have gone to the President."

"I'll get Matt over here," said the General. "He remembers just about everything. Report writing is just not my cup of tea."

The General called Matt who said he would be over in ten minutes. He was there in five minutes.

"That was fast," exclaimed the General. "You must be in a hurry to get away from someone."

"I was headed to see the Dean of Foreign Relations," answered Matt. "He was concerned over Alexi and Dimitri, and their entry into the country. I guess he does not realize that the moment the Gulfstream landed in Langley, they would automatically be U.S. citizens. He can wait. What's up?"

"This won't take long," continued the General. "Anna is concerned that every thing that needs to be said in the project report has already been covered."

"I don't think that is a problem," said Matt. "He knows that and just wants to keep the records clean. That's seems to be the way the government runs. It seems to be working pretty well. Just do a bit of cutting and pasting, and that will be good enough. The conclusion is the only thing that is important. Government reports are totally complete so the reader does not have to search previous reports. They usually include a bit of history."

"Thanks Matt," said Anna. "You are always very helpful."

"You know what they say," said Matt. "The easiest solution is often the best one."

Matt headed out the door, and the General headed upstairs to make some calls. Anna opened her MacBook Air in the downstairs den and started to work. It would not take long.

Anna was finished in no time, and forwarded the report to the General.

"Anna, that is a perfect job," said the General. "It is what we needed and wanted.

I will forward it to the President forthwith, and our project has been completed."

"Thank you Les."

"You are welcome."

THE REPORT TO THE PRESIDENT

To start with, Anna decided that the document should be confidential, but not necessarily secret. Next she thought that if the President actually read the report, he would appreciate some background material, so he could better understand what they had done. The decision making process is as important as the result. This approach essentially represented a historical view of what they had done. First and foremost, the team had to evaluate several key elements, such as:

What type of virus was it and how is it identified?
What is its source?
Where was it most prevalent?
How was it transmitted?
What are its symptoms?
What are the most common countermeasures?
How long does it last after it is diagnosed?
What is the medical community doing about it?
When the virus is gone, how long does it remain gone?
What are the conspiracy theories about it?
What organizations are involved with its treatment?
What are people actually doing about the virus?

Next, a narrative of what was going on, and what had happened so the team could understand where everyone was going with the project. Several narratives would be required. The first narrative could be called the scope of the project.

<u>Scope of the First Project</u>

It is generally felt that the virus, known a COVID-19, first entered the country on a flight from China to LAX airport in mid-March of the year 2020. The flight was far from full with 49 passengers and 8 crewmembers. In the 6-hour trip, the passengers shared restrooms, cabin air, and a narrow aisle. A retired surgeon in first class was infected with the virus, that he had contracted in January in Wuhan, China, which thoroughly disrupted the entire country, even though it was centered in Wuhan. How and why the virus spread in the U.S. so rapidly is unknown. The Chinese authorities contacted WHO – the World Health Organization - after some deliberation for supposedly political reasons. That supposition is totally unverified and is of negligible interest as far as this story is concerned. The American President referred to the COVID-19 virus as the Chinese virus, even though its origin is and was unknown. The infectious disease specialists had warned of a pandemic for more years than most people can remember. Theories on the origin of COVID-19 are many and varied. One commonly mentioned source was that COVID-19 originated from bats, and Chinese people normally eat bats. Again, this supposition is unverified. The sources rarely mentioned how a virus would affect the entire world at approximately the same time without apparent cause. In reality, cases of COVID-19 in remote locations like Bora Bora and the Canary Islands were supposedly traced to passengers arriving from other countries. Whether all of this is true or not true is not relevant to the story. The first major country to be sidelined by the virus was Italy, where the way of life was totally disrupted. Since then, most of the world has been sidelined with COVID-19, which is a fast moving disease passed through human interaction.

COVID-19 is a pandemic that took most people by surprise. History will say that it originated in China and spread from there to the rest of civilized society. The virus is highly contagious, and people were encouraged to maintain a social distance from other individuals when out in the general public and to stay indoors when possible. The wearing of face masks was advised, and many people wore gloves and protective clothing, as well. Medical supplies and first responders were in short supply, and the death rate was high for a sickness of its kind. There was no vaccine to prevent the virus, and no medicines to cure persons once they were unlucky enough to attract it.

Summary of the First Project

We are experiencing a pandemic. It is a plague.
The virus is COVD-19 and is often referred to as coronavirus.
The first outbreak of coronavirus was in China in January of 2020.
The virus spread quickly and in a few months, had spread to most countries.
The transmission has been person to person. This may not be exactly true.
It's not clear what the origin is, but many people say it is from bats, and the Chinese people eat bats. This has not been confirmed.

The general symptoms are high temperature, normally regarded as fever, dry cough, and extreme fatigue.

80% of the persons affected recover without medical treatment.

There is no vaccine or medicine for coronavirus.

The virus affects older people with underlying medical conditions and many of them die.

The incubation period is 3 to 14 days.

Precautions are wearing face masks, social distancing, and hand washing.

The motto is 'go home – stay home'. That procedure has worked with Italy, Germany, and several other countries.

Restaurants and bars have been forced to close and many persons have been laid off.

The U.S. Government has paid a financial supplement to all tax paying persons in the amount of $1600.

There has been a rush to 'open up' by business concerns, and the spread of the virus has worsened.

The hoarding of commodities has taken place. Personal difficulties are prevalent.

Practically no effort has been expended determining the origin of COVID-19.

See Addendum One

Summarization of the Second Project:

We are experiencing a pandemic. It is a plague.

The virus is COVD-19 and is often referred to as coronavirus. The term corona is intended to denote that the virus is new.

The first outbreak of coronavirus was in China in January of 2020.

The virus spread quickly and, in a few months, had spread to most countries.

The transmission has been person to person. This may not be exactly true.

It's not clear what the origin is, but many people say it is from bats, and the Chinese people eat bats. This has not been confirmed.

The general symptoms are high temperature, normally regarded as fever, dry cough, and extreme fatigue.

80% of the persons affected recover without medical treatment.

The virus affects older people with underlying medical conditions and many of them die.

The incubation period is 3 to 14 days.

Precautions are wearing facemasks, maintaining social distance, and hand washing.

The motto is 'go home – stay home'. That procedure has worked with Italy, Germany, and several other countries.

Restaurants and bars have been forced to close, and many persons have been laid off.

The U.S. Government has paid a financial supplement to all tax paying persons in the amount of $1600. Additional funds are expected.

There has been a rush to 'open up' by business concerns and the spread of the virus has worsened.

The hoarding of commodities has taken place. Personal difficulties are prevalent.

Relatively speaking, almost no effort has been expended on the origin of COVID-19, and several theories are being discussed.

See Addendum Two

Respectively submitted,

Dr. General Les Miller -- Project leader
Dr. Matthew Miller -- Technical leader
Sir Charles Bunday -- Operational management (Knight of the United Kingdom)
Hon Ashley Miller -- Analyst (Receiver of the National Medal of Freedom)
Dr. Marguerite Purgoine -- Analyst
Dr. Amelia Robinson – Analyst

Attachment:
First Addendum
Second Addendum

Addendum One: The First Report

Confidential Document
Classification: The President's Eyes Only

THE PANDEMIC

Introduction

COVID-19 is a pandemic that took most people by surprise. History will say that it originated in China and spread from there to the rest of civilized society. The virus is highly contagious, and people were encouraged to maintain a social distance from other individuals when out in the general public and to stay indoors when possible. The wearing of facemasks was advised, and many people wore gloves and protective clothing, as well. Medical supplies and first responders were in short supply, and the death rate was high for a sickness of its kind. There was no vaccine to prevent the virus and no medicines to cure persons once they were unlucky enough to attract it.

Key Elements in the Pandemic Project

What type of virus is it and how is it identified?
What is its source?
Where is the virus most prevalent?
How is it transmitted?
What are its symptoms?
What are the most common countermeasures?
How long does it last after it is diagnosed?

What is the medical community doing?
When the virus is gone, how long does it remain gone?
What are the conspiracy theories about it?
What organization is involved with its treatment?
What are people actually doing about it?

<u>Description of Pandemic Outbreak</u>

It is generally felt that the virus, known a COVID-19, first entered the country on a flight from China to LAX airport in mid-March of the year 2020. The flight was far from full with only 49 passengers and 8 crewmembers. In the 6-hour trip, the passengers shared restrooms, cabin air, and a narrow aisle. A retired surgeon in first class was infected with the virus, that he had contacted in January in Wuhan, China. The virus thoroughly disrupted the entire country of China, even though it was centered in Wuhan. How and why the virus spread in the U.S. so rapidly is unknown. The Chinese authorities contacted WHO, the World Health Organization, after some deliberation for supposedly political reasons. That supposition is totally unverified and is of negligible interest as far as this story is concerned. The American President referred to the COVID-19 virus as the Chinese virus, even though its origin was and is unknown. The infectious disease specialists had warned of a pandemic for more years than most people can remember. Theories on the origin of COVID-19 are many and varied. One commonly mentioned source was that COVID-19 originated from bats, and Chinese people often eat bats. Again, this supposition is unverified. The sources rarely mentioned how a virus would affect the entire world at approximately the same time without apparent cause. In reality, cases of COVID-19 in remote locations like Bora Bora and the Canary Islands were supposedly traced to passengers from other countries. Whether all of this is true or not true is not relevant to the story. The first major country to be sidelined by the virus was Italy, where the way of life was totally disrupted. Destroyed would be a more descriptive word. Since then, the entire world has been sidelined with COVID-19, which is a fast moving disease passed through human interaction.

Respectfully submitted,
The Pandemic Team

End of Confidential Document

Addendum Two: The Second Report

A virology laboratory has been established at a major university, and the Team has recruited an internationally known virologist as director, who is regarded as the most influential person available, and associate directors for technology and administration. Two additional issues are covered.

How Booster Vaccines Work. When a person is vaccinated with a COVID-19 vaccine shot, two distinct and important types of white blood cells are activated. The first is the plasma B cells that focus on making antibodies. This type of cell does not live very long, even though your body may be loaded with antibodies for a few weeks. If you do not get the booster in about three weeks, the antibodies go away. That is why you need a booster.

Origin Of The Coronavirus. There has been some concern over the origin of the SARS-CoV-2 virus that causes the COVID-19 virus that has infected many persons in the pandemic. Scientists from Britain and Norway claim that attempts to create a vaccine for COVID-19 will fail because the RNA sequence has elements that appear to be man-made, or artificially inserted. They claim that their vaccine Biovacc-19 will work. Many U.S. scientists claim that the COVID-19 virus is not man-made. The new U.S. recruits – Dr. Dimitri Aplov, Dr. Robert Williams, and Dr. Amelia Robinson – are specialists in that domain, and will be associated with the Ohio virology laboratory.

Monoclonal Procedure. Another open item is what do you do if you get the virus? The procedure used with the President of the U.S., former Governor, and renowned attorney is called Monoclonal Soup. It is a procedure that uses the following ingredients: Melatonin, Gilead's Remesover, Regeneron's Arktail, Zinc, Antacid, and Aspirin. The procedure is cumbersome, but it works perfectly.

END OF THE REPORT TO THE PRESIDENT

27

VISIT TO KLOSTERS

The General contacted Amelia Robinson, director of the Office of the Registrar and Associate Director of the National Virology Laboratory.

"Amelia, how are you this fine day?" asked the General. "Are you and Dimitri available for a short trip? I know you guys have been working very hard."

"We have, indeed," answered Amelia. "We have been very busy building a technical staff, and bringing the people onboard. Also, we are having an advanced lab built in a new building. Right now we are trying to recruit a technical director. He or she must be a person who is internationally known, and experienced enough to get his hands dirty in the experimental side of virology. Surprisingly, it is difficult to locate someone, even though we are willing to pay top dollar."

"I'm planning a trip to Klosters in Switzerland for our team and related people to have a little pleasure and to see how things are going," said the General.

"It sounds quite good, I must say, General," said Amelia. "Dimitri has been working 70 hour weeks. That is even a lot for Americans."

"Here is what I have planned for you, Dimitri, Matt, Ashley, Anna, and even Alexi," said the General. "You and Dimitri can take a White House jet to Langley, and we will also fly to Langley in another White House jet. I can arrange both flights. We will move the Gulfstream beforehand to Langley for routine inspection by the pilots. We will all take the Gulfstream to Kloten airport in Switzerland and then a Swiss railway to Klosters for a week of sight seeing, fine dining, and a bit of cross country skiing, if one is so interested. Lodging will be in my apartment, and accompanying facilities will be arranged. The meals will be planned in the Restaurant Chesa, across the street, where I now have a reserved table."

"That sounds fantastic," replied Amelia. "I'm glad you can arrange for the White House jets. You and the President must be real buddies."

"If you recall, we resolved his big problem – and that is not an exaggeration," said the General. "The country did not have consolidated knowledge of the pandemic situation. We provided that information, and a way of knowing so in the future, with its own national lab. Also, I will even arrange for lessons on cross-country skiing."

"Dimitri will be pleased," replied Amelia. "Dimitri knows that he needs a rest from time to time."

And so it was done. Dimitri and Amelia flew to Langley from Ohio, and the team also flew from the local airport to Langley. The meeting was extremely cordial, and the

Gulfstream was the perfect aircraft for an enjoyable flight and good conversation.

After landing at Kloten and taking a couple of taxis – actually four of them – to the Bahnhof in Zürich, the group was on its way by Swiss rail to Klosters. On the rail journey, the travellers enjoyed a snack and drink in the first class dining car. The group agreed that the Swiss really know how to live.

Everyone, except Anna, tried their hand at cross country skiing, and all had a few stiff muscles afterwards. It was great fun.

On the final day, a grand dinner was planned in the large dining room of the restaurant. The group passed the General's reserved table and was observed by a middle-aged couple.

"Excuse me, Sir," the woman said to the General. "I see you will not be using your reserved table. My husband and I would be pleased if we could use it for our dinner."

The General turned around surprised and looked at the woman. She was so sweet and her husband so gentlemanly that the General said yes and asked the Maitre D' to put their bill on his account.

"What are you sophisticated Americans doing in this fine village?" asked the General.

"My husband was a visiting professor at ETH, and we are having our last day trip before returning to the States," answered the lady.

"What does he teach?" asked the General.

"Virology," answered the woman, "There are few jobs in the States, now, because of the recession."

"Dimitri, I have someone for you to talk to," said the General."

Everyone stopped.

The gentleman and Dimitri looked at each other. They knew each other from meetings at other virology conferences.

"Dimitri," said Dr. Robert Williams.

"Robert," said Dr. Dimitri Aplov.

An amazing story unfolded. Dimitri needed exactdly what Robert was, a hands on technical director. In ensuing conversation, Dimitri hired Robert.

On the flight home in the Gulfstream, Dimitri said to the General, "Dr. General. Thank you with all of my Russian heart. America is a wonderful place to live and work."

Matt and the General were enjoying a round of golf. After the 9th hole, the General asked Matt, "I wonder what happened to Amelia and Dimitri. They have been very successful, but I wonder if Dimitri ever found out that Amelia is Russian by birth."

"We will never know," said Matt. "I wonder when a person dreams and talks in their sleep, do they it in their native language."

"We will never know," said the General. "On the subject of things we don't know, why do UFOs fly around with their lights on? Airplanes don't."

"Maybe they usually don't," said Matt. "Perhaps, the ones we see are trying to communicate with us. The universe is vast with trillions and trillions of planets. It's possible there is one just like us."

"Next, you're going to tell me they speak English," said the General.

"It's possible," said Matt with a smile on his face."

The General and Mme, Marguerite Purgoine were married in a private ceremony. Matt was the best man and Ashley was the matron of honor. The couple honeymooned in Klosters, Switzerland.

Amelia and Dimiri were apparently married, since she has taken his last name. No ceremony was announced. She is the associate director of the virology laboratory.

PART III

ADVANCED TECHNOLOGY AND THE VIRUS

28

THE AGE OF THE UFO

Matt and the General were out for their usual round of golf at the Country Club of which they were both members. The day was warm, and the breeze was light. Both were trying out the new golf balls that were supposed to spin faster and generate more distance. They had just finished the ninth hole. Neither of them was doing particularly well on this day.

"Did you see the announcement in today's news that the CIA has released a library of information on UFOs?" said Matt.

"I did," said the General. "I have something to tell you about UFOs. It's not a secret in any way, but I have not discussed it with anyone other than Buzz Bunday. Most people would not be even a little interested. Most people wouldn't know that Buzz was my wing mate, when we flew P-51s in Britain during the war."

"Fire away," said Matt. "I'm definitely interested."

"Buzz and I were out for a training run with the brand new P-51s," said the General. "It was a fast fighter in the

1940s. Buzz was my wing man. We were in constant communication during the flight. At that time, the plane was incredibly fast at more than 400 miles per hour. It was feared by the enemy. If a P-51 was on your tail, you were for sure a goner. We spotted a UFO and took off after it. Remember, we were only going 400 miles per hour. At first, it didn't see us, and we were getting close to it. Then it spotted us and took off like a shot. When we landed at the air base, we were in a little trouble for using excessive fuel. It was wartime and aviation fuel was precious. We didn't dare mention it, because the commanding officer was a real tough guy and probably would have grounded us. When we see Buzz, we could discuss the incident further."

"Well, I'll be," said Matt. "I'd like to hear more about the things you guys did during the war."

"Someday you will," said the General.

"I have a question," said Matt.

"Okay," answered the General.

"Why do UFOs always fly around with all their lights on?" asked Matt. "Maybe there are more of them flying around that we don't see."

"Could be," said the General. "But wouldn't radar reveal them."

"Maybe they are made with non-reflective materials," continued Matt.

"Probably, inquisitive people like you would drive the CIA crazy, so they decided to get out of the UFO surveillance business."

"Thanks," said Matt. "You are a good golf partner,"

29

DISCOVERING A PROBLEM

Matt and the General usually left their golf clubs in their cars, and, as a rule, each drove himself to the Country Club. Both had been busy. Matt was occupied with grading exams and assigning mid-term grades, and the General with investments that needed some attention. They hadn't spoken since they left the course three days ago.

The General asked Matt, after the 9th hole, as usual, why he had never asked about the General's recent marriage to Mme. Marguerite Purgoine, formerly a creative writing professor and an acknowledged author. She was known as Anna. Matt responded that he would know by the General's behavior if things were very good or not so good. If Matt asked the General why he had never asked the same question, the General's response was essentially the same. Life was Good, but life had been slow and quiet in the last few weeks. On the other hand, neither had been looking for anything specific to do.

The General asked about Alexi Belov, their mathematical import for the university. Alexi was a very hard worker and rarely spoke unless spoken to. He had two papers accepted for publication in a prestigious mathematical journal and had given an outstanding presentation of this math research to the faculty in the math department. Getting nothing to discuss on that subject, the General decided to approach Matt's question about the fact that UFOs always had their lights on.

"Matt, what is the latest on the UFOs, and why do they always seem to run with their lights on?" asked the General.

"I thought about it," said Matt, "and came up with an answer, a personal one, of course, that the lights had something to do with the propulsion system or the mechanism that keeps the UFO elevated. I didn't have a chance to look up the CIA documentation on the subject. The fact that there were 2780 reports on the subject gave me the feeling that they were looking for new ideas about the subject, or more probably, what the UFOs are doing that they don't know about. What about you?"

"You know that I am not all that interested in computer technology, but I did make a query on the subject," said the General. "All I entered into Google was CIA INFO DOCUMENTS, and I got a ton of information. There was this guy, Dr. Bock, who was the big gun on UFOs in Chili then Germany, but then was deported to Russia. The 'to Russia' got my attention, because that was about the time when UFOs first started being seen."

"If you put a flashlight on one of those small experimental drones," said Matt, "I would say you have a miniature UFO. I'll look up UFOs in Google and see what I can dig up."

"Can you and Ashley come for lunch one of these days?" asked the General. "Anna likes you guys and is getting tired of the Green Room"

"Ashley's classes are usually in the evening, because many of the students have full-time jobs, so she is usually free around the middle of the day," said Matt.

"When would be good?" asked the General. "How about the day after next at 1:00 pm at my house?" said the General. "Informal dress and a big appetite. Your health lunch would be appropriate on that day. I guess that is every day with you."

"Sounds like a good idea," said Matt. "It's a deal."

30

THE KICKOFF LUNCHEON

Anna welcomed Matt and Ashley as though she hadn't seen them in years. Actually, it had only been about a week. Anna had served a French salad with red wine and fried oysters. Matt and Ashley looked at each other, as if to say, what is this? The conversation at the luncheon was lively.

"I had some trouble getting my COVID-19 vaccine," said Anna. "How about you guys?"

"My university took care of it," said Matt. "I got the Pfizer vaccine, and the second shot was routine. I should have said the second jab was routine. The British have a language of their own. The first and second jabs have to be from the same manufacturer."

"How about you, Ashley?" asked Anna.

"I had to go all over New Jersey looking for one, and finally got both jabs in Atlantic City," said Ashley. "Fortunately, Matt drove. I could never find my way around that place."

"I know about the General," said Anna. "He got his jabs at the new hospital. He was a donor and took me along."

"The government really confused most people over getting the vaccine," said Matt. "People were making appointments that were cancelled because of the lack of the vaccine, even though it was supposed to be available. It seems that nobody ever knew where the vaccine went. And young people were getting it ahead of older people."

"I know," said Anna. "I met a former student on the street, who eventually went to pharmacy school. She told me her whole family – that is, extended family included – was vaccinated. She just took the shots home. But, here is what irritated me. She's Polish and the family is exceedingly large. So a large number had received those shots. I would also say that every doctor, nurse, etcetera, has been vaccinated. But here is what irritated me. Persons over 80 years of age had big trouble, even though they were in the first wave and expected to receive the vaccine. If a person were a low life, drunk, homeless, penniless – if they were in in a welfare nursing home – they got the vaccine. But a thrifty, hard working person, like a college professor who saved and lived clean, they had a terrible time getting the vaccine, even though they were also in the first wave. There should be a better way of handling a situation like this."

"I think there is," said Matt. "It is obvious and simple and doable. All levels of government have databases of citizens. Just send appointments to the persons when there time has arrived. But, in general, the question is, where has the vaccine gone."

"That's an easy one," said Ashley. "The federal government supplies the vaccine free to organizations to dispense it, also with money for doing so. The federal government pays pharmaceutical companies to do research and make the vaccine. Which organizations get the vaccine? The organizations pay someone in the government to get on the list. The organization then spins off some of the vaccine to foreign countries to provide vaccine on the sly. They use that money from the illegal sales to pay the government people, mentioned above. Who are the government people that get this payoff money? There are many examples of this. A college needs a football stadium that is paid for by the state. Who gets the job? A construction company pays someone to get the job. The persons receiving the under-the-table money are the college president and vice president. No one really knows where the money has gone, even though the process is obvious. Otherwise, how do all of these small countries get the vaccine before Americans., whose tax money paid for it."

The General said to Matt. "The business of America is business."

31

WHERE ARE THE RUSSIANS?

Matt and Ashley got up at 6:30 as usual. Both did their morning absolutions, had breakfast, and were getting ready to head out the door to their respective academic institutions. Matt got a hurried cell call from the General.

"Matt, get over here, right now, as soon as possible, no eating, no sleeping, or anything else," said the General.

"That's unusual for the General," said Matt. "Maybe, he is having a heart attach or something like that."

"I heard him," said Ashley. "You'd better get going and give me a call at the college. If you don't, I'll assume everything is okay."

Matt hurried out the door, left the garage door open, and headed to the General's house. He pulled into the circular driveway, headed inside through the unlocked front door, and into the first floor study.

The General was seated in a desk chair.

"Are you okay?" asked Matt. "Did you have a heart attack?"

"No, but I'm not okay," said the General. "Where are the Russians?"

"How should I know?" asked Matt. "They are in Ohio, and we are in New Jersey. Maybe they went on a honeymoon or something."

"The university President called over to the Virology Laboratory yesterday, and they weren't there," said the General. "Associate Director Williams said they ordered a White House jet, and that's all he knew. The university President got jumpy and called the U.S. President, who checked the White House air service, and he was told they were picked up at the local Ohio airport and taken to Newark International Airport. The university President called the local Police and was told their car was in the General Aviation parking lot. There was nothing strange or out of the ordinary. There were no Police reports on activity from or about them. The U.S. President didn't know what to do, so he called me. And I called you. He had all modes of transportation alerted. The Special Service called the airlines, all of them, and had no entries in their databases for Amelia and Dimitri Aplov. There was another couple flying to Moscow yesterday on the United Airlines 7:00 pm flight. Then I got a call from George Benson, the President's Chief of Staff, and I had no answer to the where-are-they question. So I asked you. Where do you think they went?"

"I have no idea," said Matt. "I'll look into it."

Matt left for the university and immediately went to Alexi Belov's office. Alexi was there.

"Matt," asked Alexi. "What's up? You look terrible. Have I done something wrong? I played a round of golf yesterday, during the day. Is that not okay?"

It's fine Al," answered Matt. "You can do what you please. Actually, you are a star around here. You have two papers accepted for publication, and your faculty seminar was first rate. It's something else. Amelia and Dimitri are gone. Have you heard from them?"

"I haven't seen or heard from them since they left for Ohio," said Alexi. "If Dimitri were going somewhere, he wouldn't tell me. We are not that kind of friends. All I know about them is that he is easy to get along with and likes sports."

"If he were going somewhere, do you think he would tell someone?" asked Matt.

"Of course," answered Alexi. "Russians are very careful. They are sensitive to that kind of thing. Perhaps, they are cautious because of being allies with the Americans during the war. I don't know about that. I was too young."

"Just a minute Al," said Matt. "I have to call the General." Matt called the General.

"Sir," said Matt. "I checked with Alexi Belov, and he knows nothing. He hasn't had contact with them since they left for Ohio. What about the airlines?

"The two United Airlines passengers were 60 or 70 years old," answered the General. "They had luggage, but nothing out of the ordinary. The White House jet pilots do not do luggage."

"What about a private plane?" asked Matt. "Can you ask George Benson, who is the President's right hand man?"

"The White House jet pilots," said the General, "are just military taxi drivers. They wouldn't be aware of private aircraft."

"Maybe the military drivers kidnapped them?" said Matt. "It could be for ransom."

"They are tracked by White House radar," replied the General. "I doubt that's it."

"Could they be going to the Super Bowl?" asked Matt. "Possibly one of their vendors has tickets and has access to a private plane."

"Then, why didn't the vendor's private plane pick them up in Ohio?" said the General." That doesn't sound exactly right. I'll ask George Benson to check on it. Hold on."

A few minutes later, the General called Matt in Alexi Belov's office.

"No luck, Matt." answered the General. "George Benson called the Super Bowl management and was told attendance was limited, and Amelia and Dimitri were not among the select group of the people who could attend."

"Let me call the Provost at the university in Moscow and check," said Alexi. "I can also call Dimitri's brother. I think Dimitri lived at home."

Alexi came back with the answer.

"They are not in Moscow, Matt," said Alexi. "I'm sorry, Matt, I am partly to blame for the unfortunate situation."

"No, Al," said Matt. "We are the blame, if there is any blame. We asked you to do it. Don't worry. No one in America would or will blame you. We are to blame, if there is any blame."

Matt called the General and gave him the news.

"Who is behind it, Matt?" asked the General. "You always know all the answers."

"That's not an easy question, Sir," said Matt. "We don't even know the parameters of the situation. It could be something very serious. Only Amelia could handle that. If there is any blame, we would have to look to her. Remember, we didn't choose her. The President did, and now we know who's involved in it."

"You're right there, Matt," said the General. "The U.S got its virology laboratory. So maybe as a team, we have done the equitable thing. They will show up, sometime. Case closed."

"You never know," said Matt.

32

FIGURING THINGS OUT

Matt finally decided he had had enough of Amelia and Dimitri for one day. At the last minute, he decided to visit the Dean of Foreign Relations, who was proud about bringing Alexi and Dimitri to the United States. He also had some favorable news for Matt. The importation of Alexi Belov had gone through with flying colors. Matt mentioned how good he was at supplementing the faculty in the math department. Moreover, the Dean said that Alexi Belov had, or was in the process of, receiving the planned honorariums from both the American and Russian governments in the amount of $10,000 from each government. Alexi Belov was now an official U.S. citizen. Dimitri Aplov had failed miserably, because of a criminal record, a drinking problem, and several cases of abusing women. Matt wondered if this were true, because of his knowledge of Russian men in the academic world. Dimitri Aplov definitely did not appear to be a person with a criminal record. Maybe, the Russians wanted to keep him in their clutches. The U.S. request for him was formally denied, and he did not receive neither the U.S. citizenship nor the honorariums. Yet, he was working in Ohio as though he had. Someone had pulled a few strings to get him into this country as planned. Actually, Matt had given the Dean no information, so as far as the university was concerned, it was case closed. You win some and you lose some, thought Matt.

On the way home, Matt decided to call the General to straighten things out. He called on his cell phone, and the General decided that since he was fed up with the situation and tired of being at home with bad news, that they should meet at Starbucks. Matt agreed. Matt got there first, since he knew where to park. He selected the window table.

The General arrived and gave Matt the biggest smile he had ever given him.

"Matt, you will never imagine how proud I am of you for resolving this unlikely situation, as least as far as I am concerned," said the General. "The only person who is not 100% pleased with the outcome is the university President, who was 99% pleased because he caught Dimitri Aplov drinking on the job. Perhaps, Aplov was drinking apple juice or tea. Aren't some actors and singers known to be fooling the public about their wild behavior? One guy never drank alcohol and was a family man, hitting the sack at 8:30 every night. Amelia is another thing. She will have to take what comes. She somehow got herself into this mess. Funny thing, I have some doubt about all of it. There is something wrong, and we are eventually going to find out there is a positive side to everything that has happened."

"I'm glad," said Matt. "I don't like to see you upset, even though you had good reason to be upset, or at least annoyed. I think we should make a plan for resolving the whole virus situation and getting back to our favorite pastime, and I mean regular rounds of golf."

"I'm happy to hear that," said the General.

"I have one more thing to tell you," said Matt. "I went to the office of the Dean of Foreign Affairs, and he informed me that the Alexi deal went through, and he is an official U.S. citizen and will receive the transfer money from each government in the amount of $10,000. The Dimitri Aplov deal did not. He supposedly has a criminal record, a drinking problem, and is accused of chasing women. So they say. We are really better off without him. I did not tell the Dean about today's incidents, so far as the university is concerned, it is 'case closed', and Alexi Belov is doing exceptionally well. Now, from my viewpoint, I would like to clear up the awards to Dimitri Aplov, probably handled by the U.S. and university President, and it is likely that Dimitri Aplov is now an actual U.S. citizen. I personally do not believe the charges against Dimitri, and the situation was worked out. I've also heard the contention that he drank alcohol during the day. He was for sure drinking tea, since the Russians prefer it. For alcohol, Russians prefer Vodka, and their drinking habits are likely propaganda. I would like to address the question of where the virus came from and then retire from the pandemic situation. I have some doubts above this 'missing Russians' subject."

"What about Amelia," asked the General.

"As far as I know, she did all of the recruiting and also all of the talking," said Matt. "She may be completely innocent, but I'm not sure about her. Where is she? However, she is the President's person, so we can leave it where it originated."

Matt and the General were so engaged in their conversation that they didn't even look up. When they finally did, she was there.

"I was hoping you would be here," said Ashley. "You weren't home, nor at the university, and nor playing golf, so this is where you must be."

The General and Matt told Ashley the whole story of Amelia and Dimitri, and Ashley listened intently. When they were finished, Ashley added something they didn't know.

"During our interview with Dimitri, Amelia constantly flirted with Dimitri," said Ashley. "For a criminal, drinker, and abuser, he was helpless to her attention. She wanted him in the U.S. as much as he wanted to be here. It's strange that we don't know where she is. This reminds me of the Prince Michael affair."

"Anyway," said the General. "We are here to discuss where we want to go with the virus business. I should have said pandemic. Maybe, it will turn into an endemic."

"I think it's too early for discussing an endemic," said Ashley. "We don't even know where they are. We don't know how well they have done at the Virus Lab. They could be down the street visiting someone. Perhaps, they have been captured by the Russians and hidden away in the mountains somewhere in Maine. Maybe, they are on drugs. There are plenty of drugs around a college campus."

"She's right," said Matt. "We can't pull out yet. Maybe not ever."

"I suppose you are both correct," said the General. "I'm getting the feeling there is more to the story than we originally realized."

"So we have to do what we have to do," said Matt. "Our team is depleted beyond recognition."

"We have the three of us, plus Anna and Buzz," said Ashley. "Buzz may be unable to work with us now that he is a Sir, and Anna probably doesn't like the active part of our work. I could be wrong, but that is a start."

"We can build a team," said Matt. "But first, we have to determine what we have to do."

"The basis of our work is still the origin of the COVID-19 virus," replied the General. "Why are we interested in it, in the first place?"

"From my viewpoint, if the virus is man-made and we don't knock it out, it will undoubtedly reappear," said Ashley. "If it is natural, then we have to know how to control it. If it is from outer space, then we have work to do. When Michael was doing astrophysics, he saw something very suspicious. Maybe he saw UFOs in the telescopes. His colleagues didn't believe him and thought he was bonkers. Maybe, all of this is related to the UFO occurrences. There were a lot of them, and recently, the CIA, through the freedom of information act, released something like 2780 reports or pages - I don't exactly know what - on UFOs. The UFOs may be under the jurisdiction of the U.S., and they may not be related to our problem. But, maybe they are. We should talk to Michael, because he really believed in the outer space theory, and no one would believe him. Okay, he has an attitude, but that doesn't really matter. Sorry, I can't help you anymore on that end. It is possible that the UFOs from outer space are carrying the virus."

"Don't be too sure that you can't help with Michael," said Matt to Ashley. "But, I couldn't say how at this point."

"I'm wondering about this Dimitri," said the General. "We should ask Alexi about Dimitri's drinking," said the General. "It could be apple juice. Remember that bunch of performers in Las Vegas that had a reputation of drinking a lot and playing around. As it turns out, one of the main guys actually drank apple juice and was a good family man. Went to sleep at 8:30 every night. Perhaps, our university President jumped to the wrong conclusion."

"We should check with the associate director, the scientist named Robert Williams or William Roberts, that we all met in Klosters," said Matt. "We should ask him specifically about Dimitri and Amelia. We have a lot to do before we start doing what we should be doing."

"His name is Robert Williams," said the General. "Matt, I'm sure you wouldn't mind running our project. I'm going to contact the U.S. President to determine if he will finance this operation. If he doesn't agree, then I'll do it personally. I don't anticipate any more last minute trips to the White House."

33

ALMOST TOO BUSY FOR GOLF

It was a cold and windy Saturday morning, but the two golfing partners were at it again. The fairways and greens were dry and that was all that mattered to Matt and the General. After the ninth hole, as usual, the General requested Matt's attention. By the way, the restrooms were after the ninth hole.

"We haven't played a round lately,' said the General. "What have you been up to? The last time we talked, you were into the math of strings and black holes."

"I've been working on artificial intelligence, AI as they call it," said Matt. "When I was a graduate student, I sat in on a set of lectures by a guest professor in the Computer Science Department. So I bought his AI book, and I have been working my way through it. It has a lot of pages. It touches on just about everything."

"What is AI?" asked the General.

"It's artificial intelligence, that is doing by computers what is normally done by a person," answered Matt.

"Is it like doing the payroll?" asked the General. "I guess that is too simple. Is it like reading and writing or playing games?"

"It's about doing complicated things, but does include games. In the early days of computers, a scientist at IBM wrote a program that can play checkers. Things have progressed since then. Now, computers can play chess, understand speech, and read books. It kind of began in 1956 when a group of scientists met at Dartmouth College in Hanover, New Hampshire over summer break to discuss doing important intellectual things by computer. They couldn't agree for a name for it, until John McCarthy thought up the name artificial intelligence. McCarthy was working at Dartmouth at the time and eventually migrated to Stanford University. A good short definition is a computer that can perform tasks normally associated with human intelligence."

"Can a computer fly an airplane?" asked the General.

"Most of the recently built commercial airliners can land by themselves without a pilot's intervention," said Matt. "Modern AI involves learning and reasoning more complicated than landing an airplane. Maybe in the near future, the military will have fighter planes with no flight pilots, because the planes are flown by AI."

Matt smiled.

"I like the old way better," replied the General.

"Maybe UFOs are flown by AI," said Matt.

"That would be nice," added the General sarcastically. "Before long, we won't need people."

"Some people are worried about that," added Matt.

"How about you?" asked the General.

"I haven't thought about it that much," answered Matt. "Could be."

"Let's get going," said The General. "I have to go to Washington."

"The White House?" asked Matt.

"No, the Pentagon," aid the General. "And I have to dress up, but I get a special plane ride."

"Better you than me," responded Matt.

This would be the last round of golf for a while, but the golfers did not know it.

As they left the Country Club, Matt asked the General about Klosters.

"The General replied, "Haven't been there since we went as a team with the Russians. Want to go for vacation?"

"No, but thanks," said Matt. "Right now, I seem to be busy, doing essentially nothing."

34

ASHLEY'S CONTRIBUTION

"You said we were going to work on the origin of the virus," said Ashley. "I don't see any big progress."

"I suppose that everyone involved is too busy or doesn't care or is working in secret," answered Matt. "When you get finished, you don't have to write one of those super-duper reports you are known for coming up with – just tell me what you have come up with."

"I'll not make it a complete report, but I will make one of my lists of subjects," said Ashley. "Then if you're nice, I'll tell you about it, because you don't seem to like that kind of stuff. You only like long equations and that kind of thing."

Ashley proceeded as usual by making a list, and then followed with a verbal discussion. **Here is what she dictated into her iPhone:**

Options
    Man-made
    Natural
    From outer space
Man-made
    Bioweapon
    Humanitarian
Natural
    How
    Where
Man-made questions
    How and when
    Reasons
    Who
Natural
    Built into to the human condition
    Not in world Earth
    How it works
Outer space
    How it gets here
    Where from
    Why do it in the first place

The key question is whether the virus was man-made or natural. Then, if it was man-made, who made it, where, and how did it get spread so readily all over the world at about the same time. It could be natural and spread all over the world at the same time, but how? If it were a virus made by a person or a group, why did they do it? It could be a bioweapon or some crazy group with the idea of reducing the population by killing off old people. In grammar school, the teachers tell you the Eskimos did just that after the women became old and useless. They were placed on a floating iceberg and pushed out to sea. If it were a bioweapon, who would want to do it? Not likely people from Russia or China. It could be made by one country and used be another.

Some people are thinking the virus came from bats, and Chinese people eat bats. That's why they call it the Chinese virus. Live bats are sold and purchased in the fresh-food markets. The virus might come from the feces of bats. It doesn't seem like the vast number of viruses could come from a bunch of 2-inch bats that live in caves and in the rafters of farmer's barns. All you would have to do is to go all over the world setting fire to the bat caves. A lot of this information comes from the World Health Organization (WHO). But you can't trust them. Give them a few million, and they will say they have definite proof for about anything. Another possibility is deforestation. It is said the bat virus jumps from bats to animals. With deforestation, the viruses jump from bats to people. Voila, a pandemic. Now, if the virus were man made, who and why and when and where. **___Now, the following is___ ___important.___** *Prince Michael said he observed* *some phenomena emanating from outer space. It appeared to be coming from another planet in another galaxy. He happened to use astrophysics cameras on the wrong data. That could be another planet, just like mother Earth. Because of the billions of planets in our universe, it is often said there is a high probability that there is a planet just like ours. This is a little repetitious, but I am in a hurry. Maybe a planet is going extinct, and they want to put their people and other things on Earth. All of those UFOs are just checking us out. Why not? Send over a lot of viruses and kill us all off. Then move in. For those of you reading this, you should talk to Matt. He is a master with complicated things.*

Respectfully submitted,
Ashley Miller

Matt got Ashley's report and sent it to the General. He was totally amazed. Matt printed it out on his wireless printer – two copies – one for himself and one for the General. Matt was in the process of advising his PhD candidate and showed him a copy. The student read it in haste and then again, slowly, and said to Matt.

"I agree with your associate totally, Dr. Miller. There is supposed to be a planet in the Pinwheel Galaxy that has the physical characteristics of earth. My brother is an Astronomy Professor at Harvard and is always telling me some interesting fact like that."

Matt went directly home after his office hours were finished and forwarded the second copy of Ashley's report to the General. The General thought that the overall approach was very good but would be interested in additional information on the galaxy phenomena. Matt was a little disappointed with the lack of enthusiasm on the part of the General, until he said, "I'm more than interested in the idea about another galaxy being responsible for the basic COVID-19 pandemic."

Matt knew they were on their way to a very interesting problem and an even more interesting solution. It was no longer a situation, but a solution.

"I really can't help you very much on this one," said Matt. "As you know, my specialty is mathematics. I think you should contact Sir Buzz and ask him to have a serious talk with Prince Michael. I think you would be well off, but I can see a possible problem with Anna. If you went to London, it would be protocol to meet with Katherine Penelope Radford."

"Why is that?" asked the General. "Because it would be expected that you, being a four-star General and she being the retired but former Queen, both leaders of your respective countries, to meet during your visit."

"I see," said the General. "You know Matt, after all these years, I know better than to get involved with another woman, especially when that woman is a retired Queen, but I do admit that the British media would love it."

"I have an idea," said Matt.

"I can always count on you to find an answer to a tough problem," said the General with a big smile. The General liked the solution that Matt would deliver, before he heard it.

"Here it is," said Matt. Please don't laugh at me if you don't like it."

"It is possible that I wouldn't like it, but I would never laugh at you," answered the General.

"Michael has been unusually reluctant about telling about just what he spotted in the States, and at which the others on his team laughed," said Matt. "Then, he went back to London, and they said he was bonkers. I doubt that you, Sir Buzz, or I, can get anything out of him. The person who could is Mum, his mother and retired Queen, to whom he is truly devoted. I would suggest that you and Buzz meet with her to set up a meeting. The retired Queen will understand why you can't take her on one of your famous dates."

"The retired Queen's name is Katherine Penelope Radford," said the General, "Let's call her Radford. As to the question at hand, it could work."

"I could work it out with Anna," replied Matt. "She will probably recommend that you do something with Katherine Penelope Radford. She's a grand dame. It's hard to call one's favorite professor by her last name."

"She got it from the Royal Lexicographer," said the General. "I'll try to work it out as soon as possible. You are a good associate, Matt. You are the best."

"Thanks," said Matt. He was very pleased.

The General used his satellite phone to call Buzz. Buzz answered on the first ring.

"How's it going, Sir Buzz?" asked the General.

"Same as ever," answered the General's Army buddy, Buzz, now known as Sir Charles Bunday, Knight of the Royal Kingdom. "As I mentioned in our last call, being a Knight is not what it is cranked up to be."

"Perhaps, I can help you out in that regard," answered the General. "We're looking into the origin of the COVID-19 virus and not doing so well. It appears to be an elusive subject."

"I'm sure that it is," replied Buzz. "Our Prince Michael professes that it comes from outer space. After a short career in America as an astrophysicist, he is now regarded as being bonkers, and won't speak to anyone on that subject, including me. I doubt he would speak to you either."

"How about his Mum, the former Queen, now known as Katherine Penelope Radford?" asked the General. "Apparently, she convinced him to leave the States and return to the royal scene in London."

"That sounds like a clever idea, Les," replied Buzz. "All you have to do is get over here and talk to her. She admires you and was impressed when you gave her a credit card. How did you put a limit on it?"

"That was easy, Buzz," said the General. "All I did was to ask the credit card company to put on it an expiration data of two months in the future. Actually, she never charged anything."

"You're quite a guy, Les," said Buzz. "You probably know there is a renewed interest in UFOs."

"I do know," said the General. "Can you set up an appointment with her and while we are there in London together, we can discuss the renewed interest in UFOs. We do have a unique perspective."

"I'll set it up for a few days from now, unless she is on holiday in Balmoral Castle," said Buzz. "I'll get back to you. What about your new wife?"

"I'll have to think about that," said the General. "Depending on who is with me, we might want to spend a day or two as tourists. We could see the Mousetrap play, even though I know the conclusion."

"I'll call you back," said Buzz, "when I have some results."

They both hung up. It was like their Army days as P-51 pilots.

35

PLANS FOR LONDON

"Matt, would you like to visit London?" asked the General. "I'll pay your way."

"I don't need money," answered Matt, "and I know for sure you have something in mind."

"I'm interested in what Prince Michael has to say about outer space, but I doubt that I can do it personally. So, I'm thinking about asking the retired queen to do it."

"She will do anything for you, Sir." Said Matt. "You opened up her life for her."

"I did," said the General. "She's a magical person, who represented her country and empire for many years with dignity. We always had pleasant times together."

"What about Anna banana?" asked Matt. "That's how we referred to her when we were students. She knew it, but never said a thing. Will she be jealous?"

"That's why I called you," replied the General.

"I'll ask Ashley," said Matt. "She loves problems. This one is right down her alley."

"'The simplest answer is always the best'," said the General. "I guess we'll never forget it."

"I got a call from the President," said Matt.

"You did," said the General attentively. "What did he want? Is his wife lost again?"

"She's a nice lady," said Matt. "Being a First Lady is a difficult job, and she is constantly in the national spotlight. He asked if I knew what happened to Amelia and Dimitri."

"What did happen to them?" asked the General. "Did they go back to Russia?"

"You know I don't have a clue," said Matt. "I said I didn't know, and that was it. He hung up without a word."

"Will you be going with us to London?" asked the General.

"Depends on when and for how long," answered Matt.

"I don't know for sure, but I can figure it out," said the General. "Depends on Radford's meeting with the Prince, that is if he agrees to it. There will be some free time. Here's what I guess. I'm jotting it down as I speak. Fly to London on Sunday, and then the following agenda:

Meet with the retired Queen – 1 day
Retired Queen meets with Prince Michael – 1 day
Retired Queen meets with Buzz and me – 1 day
Retired Queen has a pleasure day with me – 1 day

That's 4 days, Monday through Thursday. We have a free day on Friday and fly back to the States on Saturday."

"Okay," said Matt. "Who is going?"

"That's why I called you," answered the General.

"I'll call you this evening," said Matt.

Ashley returned home from her afternoon at the college and was greeted by Matt with anticipation.

"We have an important problem for you," said Matt.

"Who is 'we'?" said Ashley.

"The General and me," replied Matt.

"Oh," said Ashley. "I was hoping for something challenging all afternoon and was really anxious to get home. I thought that working girls came home, kicked off their heels, and had a glass of white wine."

"Sounds like you need a Green Room filet," said Matt.

"I had hoped you would say that," answered Ashley, with a mischievous smile.

The couple got a choice table at the Green Room, and after getting settled, Ashley asked, "Please, what is your important question?"

"It's this way," gegan Matt. "We are on the trail of where the virus came from, and the General needs to know what Michael has to say, and Michael isn't talking. The general is working with Buzz on this. Michael won't tell anything to Buzz either. Remember, Michael is sensitive to requests from his Mum, Katherine Penelope Radford, who is the retired Queen. So the General and Buzz made this plan that the General will tell the retired Queen what he wants, and she will ask Michael, who will give a decent answer to her. She would then relay the requested information to the General and Buzz. Now here is the start of the situation that we class as a problem. Remember the General took the retired Queen on a couple of outings, which included going to Harrods, the Ritz for a drink, and then Simpson's on the Strand for dinner. She would probably expect the same this time. Now here's the problem, or question if you wish to phrase it that way. Would Anna be jealous and how should he inform her of the situation? We have some free time in London when we are there that includes the General, you, me, Sir Buzz, and maybe Anna. Should we invite Anna, and who would inform her of the innocent situation. Or, should not tell her at all."

"That's an easy problem to solve," said Ashley. "The General should just tell Anna what he plans to do, and that she can come along, because of the free time. Actually, only the General and Buzz will be occupied at all because of the nature of the operations. Anna can choose whether she would like to come along with us, if she wanted to. That's the most straightforward solution. If she doesn't agree, then she can lump it and stay here."

"That simple?" asked Matt.

"That simple," replied Ashley. "She will go to London and enjoy every minute of it, including the shopping at Harrods and the fine dining."

"In other words, the General has just to inform Anna as to what he has to do, and that's it," said Matt. "Ashley, you're the best."

"I know it," said Ashley. "But it's nice to hear it every once in a while. Can I come too?"

"Of course," said Matt. "I wouldn't leave home without you."

As Matt and Ashley left the Green Room, a couple, sitting nearby, noticed their casual manner. The woman said, "That tall suntanned man sure picked a nice-looking woman. I wonder if she is a movie star." Her husband replied, "He is the owner of that Porsche Taycan out in front. If a man can choose a beautiful car, he can also choose a beautiful woman."

When Matt and Ashley got home, Matt relayed Ashley's opinion about Anna and the retired Queen to the General.

The General replied, "The simplest solution is often the best solution. That wife of yours is really something."

36

LONDON BUSINESS

Buzz called the General and told him the meeting with Katherine Penelope Radford, the retired Queen, was set for the following Monday at 9:00 am in her royal residence in the Palace. The meeting would include the General, Sir Charles Bunday, known as Buzz by the General, and the retired Queen. Buzz mentioned the subject of the meeting, and the retired Queen understood perfectly and scheduled a meeting with herself and Prince Michael for Tuesday at 9:00 am.

The retired Queen scheduled another meeting with the General and Buzz on Wednesday to go over Tuesday's results. The retired Queen was sharp as a whip and understood practically everything that took place in the United Kingdom. She asked if the General would be free on Thursday, and Buzz replied that he would be. This schedule afforded some leisure time on Friday before the return flight to the States on Saturday. London was still in the midst of a lock down so landing rights at the Royal Air Force base was secured. A limo for the duration of the trip was ordered for the team. Sir Charles asked to be advised of the team's schedule in order to schedule the time to be available at the Air Force base. He also mentioned that he would be in the limo so that plans for the upcoming conversation with the retired Queen could be adequately planned. An executive suite would also be secured at a first class hotel, as well as reserved tickets for the Mousetrap play. The reservation for the latter could be cancelled, if necessary. And, that was it. The team was practically on its way. The last item was Anna.

"Anna, I have something to ask you?" asked the General.

"Go ahead," said Anna. "You have never asked before."

"The team has to go to London, and I wonder if you would like to go. It will be a pleasure trip for you, Matt, and Ashley. Prince Michael has information we need, and Buzz and I are involved."

Anna hesitated a second, then said, "Les, it is okay if you meet with the retired Queen. Don't be concerned. I am a mature woman and realize that you have to do what is necessary. You don't have to ask me to go with you. But, I would enjoy a visit to London. Will Ashley and Matt be coming with us?"

"They are," said the General. "Welcome aboard."

The meetings were arranged. All the General had to do was arrange for the pilots and have the Gulfstream 650

available at Newark International. The team would take a local limo to the airport.

The flight to London was high and fast, and the General called Buzz in route with the requested time of arrival. When they arrived at the British Air Force base north of London, the limo was waiting for the team's short ride to the luxury lodging for the team. It was the Savoy Hotel, and Buzz told the General that the limo would pick him up at 8:30 am. As expected, Buzz would be with him.

As of Sunday evening, all was well. The team had a light dinner in the holel and retired early.

The limo was available at 8:30 am and, shortly afterwards, Buzz and the General were ushered into the retired Queen's suite at Buckingham Palace at 9:00 am, as scheduled. There were no British or even American hugs this morning. Only, handshakes were offered and accepted.

"Well, I'm not sure why you are here, but I've made a good guess," said Madam Katherine Penelope Radford, a name suggested by the Royal Lexicographer, for the retired Queen. You would like information from Prince Michael, and he won't talk. Am I correct?"

"It is, indeed," said the General. "We are investigating the sources of the COVID-19 pandemic, Nd feel that the Prince Michael has information that we need. That information is important for the continued success of the free world, as we know it today. There are only two questions. The first is how did Michael obtain the information he knows, and secondly, precisely what information did he uncover. We recognize he was treated unfairly in the U.S., but that is something we were not a party to."

"Very well, I will do the best I can," said Radford. "I would like to invite you gentlemen to a private tour of Buckingham Palace, one that tourists never experience, followed by a special royal luncheon for the three of us."

The offer was accepted, and the first day's work for the General and Buzz was finished.

It was Tuesday, and Prince Michael met with his Mum, the retired Queen. They were close friends beyond their respective roles. They started with a warm hug. The retired Queen was the person that convinced Michael to pursue his studies in astrophysics at Oxford University, where he received his PhD and achieved worldwide acclaim as an astrophysics scholar.

"Why am I here, Mum?" asked Michael. "Have I done anything I shouldn't have done?"

"You have done nothing inappropriate, Michael. You are my favorite son, and the most admired person in England and probably elsewhere, as well. I will tell you only the truth. What we have to do is important for the British Empire. Will you help us?"

"I will do anything you wish, Mum," said Michael.

"When you were director of the Astrophysics Laboratory, you experienced an event that is important," said Madam Bradford. "Can you tell me what it was?"

"Yes, it started out as a simple equipment error," answered Michael. "I was going to use an astrophysics electron camera and focused it at a close distance rather than a far distance. It was a common error, as I was not accustomed to using the equipment. In the United States, that is commonly done by technicians."

"Then, what happened?" asked Madam Radford.

"I viewed a large squadron of space vehicles headed for Earth. There was a very high number of them, and they appeared to be in complete synchronicity, probably driven by one computer or by individual computers operating in exactly the same way. The formations were without any deviation."

"Is that all," asked Madam Radford.

"Some of them were lighted, such as UFOs normally are," said Michael.

"Anything else?" asked Madam Radford.

'Yes," said Michael. "I focused the electron camera outward and observed that the squadron was emanating from within another galaxy."

"It appeared to be from the Pinwheel Galaxy that has a planet Zenex with identical characteristic to Earth. The lighted UFOs appeared to be leaders, and the others could be controlled by artificial entities. I mentioned the event or events, I'm not sure, to my American associates and they ridiculed me and said I was crazy and dreaming things. That is why I mentioned returning to the Monarchy to you."

"Is that all there was to it?" asked Madam Radford.

"It was just that simple," replied Michael.

"Would you like to have a luncheon or a meeting with Sir Charles and General Miller?" asked Madam Radford.

"I think not, Mum," said Michael. "I am very happy with my position at Oxford and my work on the COVID-19 vaccine and my position in the Monarchy."

"Thank you, Michael," said Madam Radford. "You know that I and the Monarchy are extremely proud of you."

Madam Radford called Sir Charles and arranged a meeting at 8:00 am the next day for an English breakfast. She had a Royal transcriptionist prepare a summary of the result of the conversation with Michael. Sir Charles and the General had received the information they had come for. On the limo ride from the palace, Sir Charles remarked, "an unlikely situation".

The Monarch Style English breakfast was a distinct pleasure. Madam Radford asked the General if he was available on Thursday, the next day, for one of their favorite dates, and the General said he was.

The next day, Madam Radford and the General had a joyous visit to Harrods, the Ritz, and Simpson's on the Strand restaurant. The General and the retired Queen, the Madam Radford, had a grand time and they agreed to do it again, if the situation presented itself.

The team had an enjoyable day off on Friday, and the seats in the Royal Box for the famous Mousetrap play, were excellent. Both Ashley and Matt knew the final result, and the others did not speak of it as that is the custom. The Mousetrap play, written by Agatha Christie has run for more than fifty consecutive years in London. The Americans complimented the London theatre, because it was large enough to know it's for a play, but small enough to see the actors. Some English people bring a box of chocolates, and after a couple of pieces pass the box on. Christie said she would not write a book on the Mousetrap, but she did. In the Matt and the General's initial book, entitled the Mysterious Case of the Royal Baby, the name of the book is given. As a student, Ashley had a part in that play.

On the flight home, the team discussed the meeting with Michael. Only Ashley and Matt thought the analysis of Michael's description was feasible.

Someone asked the question of how could one of those UFOs with the lights would work. Matt gave an answer without a second's thought.

"Here's how my thinking progressed," said Matt. "I don't suppose you remember that in the 1950s, the Army somehow got hold of a UFO and took it to Area 51 in Nevada. We've never heard anything about it. I mean the general public. Funny thing, the Boeing Airplane Company, now called just Boeing, had a project to develop a Closed Ecological System (CES) sponsored by the Defense Department. The cold war was upon us, and this was one of the options to survival. Ina CES, humans could live for an extended period in an enclosure containing water, plants, and a crop of fish. The humans could eat the fish. The plants could absorb the carbon monoxide, and so forth. The system was actually built at Boeing and tested there. People could survive for an extended period of time. I never heard what happened to the project. The UFOS with lights could be surveying the planet Earth and return to the Pinwheel Galaxy in a CES, even though it's pretty far. They could have special aircraft."

"I've heard it's about 21 million light years away," said Ashley.

"What's a light year?" asked Anna.

"A light year is the distance that light can travel in a year," said Sir Charles Bunday, who was traveling to the States with his wife in preparation for a short vacation in Klosters, Switzerland.

"To continue." said Matt. "Then space ships, piloted by artificial intelligence systems and using nuclear power could be distributing phenomena, such as the COVID-19 virus, to the entire world. When we are all killed, the inhabitants of their planet in Pinwheel Galaxy, which is going extinct, could be transferred to Earth through a large number of CESs in space ships powered by nuclear engines and controlled by artificial intelligence."

"That scares me," said the General.

"It could happen, and there is a chance it has already started," replied Matt.

The passengers were all quiet – extremely so.

"The meeting we had with Prince Michael," said the General, "confirms that concept. This was a very important business trip."

"General, can't the military stop this," asked Mrs. Bunday.

"It may be an endemic," said the General. "We would have to repeat our effort each year – approximately."

"It would be very difficult for the people in our country to continue the practice of face masks, social distancing, and hand washing in addition to social conditioning," said Matt. "Take it from me, however, that we will solve the problem. The United States always does."

37

LOCATING THE MISSING VIROLOGISTS

During the flight from London to Newark International Airport, the General called Jacques, the Māitre d' at the Chesa Grischuna restaurant in Klosters via his satellite phone.

"Jacques, this is the General."

"Yes Sir, General," the Māitre d' responded. "How can I help you?"

"Can you please step across the street and check my apartment. I'm having some friends stay there for a week or so, and I would like to make sure everything is ship shape."

"Hold on, General," said Jacques. "I'll be back in 5 minutes."

Jacques returned in 15 minutes.

"General, there is a couple there," said Jacques. "They introduced themselves as Dr. Dimitri Aplov and Dr. Amelia Aplov. They said they were associated with the United States Government, and they have permission to stay in your apartment for a couple of weeks. Shall I have them removed?"

"No, Jacques," replied the General. "I'll take care of it. Thank you. You will have a bonus on your salary."

"Thank you, Sir," said the Māitre d'. "Is that all, Sir?"

"Yes, Jacques," answered the General. "How is the weather in Klosters?"

"It is always beautiful here," said the Māitre d'. "Please return to us as soon as you can."

The General motioned for Matt to come over to an accompanying seat.

"Matt, I have located the missing persons," said the General. "They are in my apartment in Klosters."

"Well, I'll be," said Matt.

The General called the President.

"Hello, Les, what can I do for you?" asked the President. "I see you are in flight, ostensibly flying back to the States."

"How do you know that?" asked the General.

"We know everything, Les," said the President. "Actually, we got it from the satellite locator connected with the satellite call you made."

"We have located your missing scientists," said the General. "They are residing in my apartment in Klosters."

"Did you give them permission?" asked the President,

"I have had no contact with them in any way, shape, or form," replied the General.

"That is why they couldn't be found," said the President. "They didn't try very hard to hide out."

"They probably wanted to be found," said the General. "They know something that they think other people would like to know, but the university environment is not the place to present it to the world. If they were well known, that is, if they had a lot of publications and associates, it would be a different story. They do not know what to do."

"Okay Les," said the President. "I will get them here, and if you can bring your team, I think we can accomplish something. Here is what to do. Bring your team here. I mean the White House. I will get the two lost souls here also, and we'll work it out. That means, exactly and precisely what to do under the current circumstance."

"If you can have a White House jet at Newark International, we will come there directly. Can you get us a room?"

"We will take care of everything," said the President, "I will see you here the day after tomorrow. You will be advised of all other times and events. I have to go."

The General advised the team that they were headed to the White House, and there was not a complaint from anyone."

The President called in George Benson, his Chief of Staff.

"George, take a C2 White House jet, and three Special Service Agents, one of them a female, to Klosters, Switzerland. Bring the two Russians staying there to DC and have them lodged in the Mayflower Hotel, under an invisible guard – one that preserves his or her identity. Make it the two or three that went to Switzerland. They are in

General Miller's apartment across the street from the Chesa Grischuna Restaurant/Hotel located at 7 Bahnhofstrasse. Make no threats and be as cordial as possible, but tell them nothing. Bring them to the White House in the morning on the day after tomorrow.

38

AN UNCOMPARABLE DISCOVERY

The participants were ushered into the President's conference room. There was water, paper, and special point pens at each place. The President, Kenneth Strong, sat in the middle with George Benson on his right. The general, Les Miller, was on his left. Matt Miller sat across from the President, and Ashley was at Miller's right. Mme. Purgoine sat to Matt's left. The invited guest, Sir Charles Bunday, sat next to the General, and Amelia and Dimitri Aplov sat across from the General.

"We all know each other and why we are here, said the President. We are here to determine the source of the COVID-19 virus. The reasons of economics, weaponry, and political power have been investigated. There is one remaining source in which we are interested: outer space. Matt, can you bring us up to date?"

"Thank you, Mr. President," said Matt. "I will do that just as briefly as possible. The initial interest in outer space originated from our astrophysics laboratory in New Jersey.

There was unexpected action coming from the Pinwheel Galaxy and planet Zenex. It had physical characteristics that are the same as Earth. UFOs have been of interest to Americans and people from other countries. We find that UFOs with lights could be searching the U.S. and other countries using replenishable solar energy for propulsion and the known system for life support named Closed Ecological System (DES) to allow persons to travel from Zenex and return. The distance is great but the technology supports it. For participants, time slows down as we approach the speed of light. The planet Zenex is going extinct, and it is hypothesized that they want to extinguish life on Earth and relocate here. A killer agent, namely virus technology, has been initiated – as we all know. There can be two kinds of UFOs. The first is lighted and transports and supports human occupants. Thee can be a dark UFO that initiates the virus attack that is computer driven, i.e., no pilot, using artificial intelligence that can be destroyed after the payload has been released. They blow themselves up over the ocean. The Ohio virological team has supported the above conjecture using similar methods. There are other aspects to this theory, but this is the essence of it."

"The Ohio virological team supports this position through established virological research," said Dimitri Aplov.

"Are there any comments?" asked the President.

There were no additional responses.

"Well, let me fill you in," said the President. "The Defense Group and the U.S. Defense Team have planned a new military force. It is named the SPACE FORCE, and there will be an official announcement in two days. It should protect planet Earth and the United States against spatial invasion of any king."

On the flight in a White House jet to New Jersey, the General said to the team. "We preserved the sanctity of the United States and planet Earth. We should be proud. We did our job. Case closed."

A BRIEF AFTERWARD

As in real life, a person often wonders what has happened to friends or acquaintances. In this case, the COVID-19 virus would also be of interest. So here goes.

Matt and the General are the same. They manage to get at least two rounds of golf in each week, except when they are playing exceptionally well, it is three. The only exceptions are when the General is in Klosters, Switzerland with Anna.

Ashley has become a noted author and usually produces two books in a calendar year. She is now chairman of the drama department. Anna is enjoying being a jet setter, along with the General.

The pandemic has subsided, that is, for those countries that have adopted the American vaccines. The Ohio Virological Laboratory turned out to be a tremendous success and is a model for other countries.

Sir Charles Bunday and his wife enjoy spending as much time as possible with Anna and the General in Klosters.

Finally, Prince Michael, Knight of the Royal Kingston, finally received the credit for his hard work that he truly deserved.

PS: The U.S. Space Force now serves as a model for the world, but their work is highly classified.

Thanks for reading the book.

ABOUT THIS BOOK

This book is a novel that was written solely for entertainment. The characters, places and events are all the product of the author's imagination. Of course, events and places with the same name, do in fact, exist but not necessarily in the manner given. Those entities are created to serve the plot of the story. For example, the purchase of a residence in Switzerland by a foreigner and the operation of a Russian air base are totally for enjoyment.

Most of the included information on viruses and related phenomena are essentially true, but possibly out of date in some cases.

The team consisting of Matt, the General, Ashley, and Anna does not exist in real life, except by an extreme coincidence.

The flights of the General's Gulfstream 650 are a bit exaggerated but could actually happen. The manner in which money is disbursed is not at all true and used for entertainment.

The information on planets, galaxies, UFOs, and complex ecological systems is largely true but may be exaggerated in some cases. The methods of artificial intelligence are true for the most part, but an interested reader should refer to a textbook for further information.

In summary, the book is a made-up collection of people and events that aren't true, and the conclusion hasn't happened. But you never know, it could end up being true.

The author would like to thank his wife Margaret for helping with the manuscript.

This book adheres to the author's policy of no sex, no violence, and no bad language.

ABOUT THE AUTHOR

Harry Katzan, Jr. does exist and is a professor who has written several books and peer-reviewed technical papers on computer science and service science. He is a business consultant and has been the founder and the editor of the Journal of Service Science. He enjoys running and has completed many races, including the Boston Marathon 13 times and the New York City Marathon 14 times. He has worked for Boeing and IBM and he and his wife have lived in Switzerland where he was a visiting professor. He holds bachelors, masters, and doctorate degrees.

THE DISCOVERY

Adventures of Matt and the General

HARRY KATZAN JR.

Printed in the United States of America.

Library of Congress Control Number: 2022950971

ISBN	Paperback	978-1-68536-977-4
	Hardback	978-1-68536-979-8
	eBook	978-1-68536-978-1

Westwood Books Publishing LLC
Atlanta Financial Center
3343 Peachtree Rd NE Ste 145-725
Atlanta, GA 30326

www.westwoodbookspublishing.com

For Margaret, as always

Made in the USA
Columbia, SC
14 March 2023

13736162R00115